the small room

Books by May Sarton

POETRY

Encounter in April
Inner Landscape
The Lion and the Rose
The Land of Silence
In Time Like Air
Cloud, Stone, Sun, Vine
A Private Mythology
As Does New Hampshire
A Grain of Mustard Seed
A Durable Fire
Collected Poems, 1930–1973
Selected Poems of May Sarton
(edited by Serena Sue Hilsinger and Lois Byrnes)

NOVELS

The Single Hound
The Bridge of Years
Shadow of a Man
A Shower of Summer Days
Faithful Are the Wounds
The Birth of a Grandfather
The Fur Person
The Small Room
Joanna and Ulysses
Mrs. Stevens Hears the Mermaids Singing
Miss Pickthorn and Mr. Hare
The Poet and the Donkey
Kinds of Love
As We Are Now
Crucial Conversations
A Reckoning

NONFICTION

I Knew a Phoenix
Plant Dreaming Deep
Journal of a Solitude
A World of Light
The House by the Sea

the small room

room

A NOVEL BY

MAY SARTON

W · W · NORTON & COMPANY · INC · NEW YORK

The Norton Library

Books That Live
The Norton Imprint on a book means that in the publisher's
estimation it is a book not for a single season but for the years.
W. W. Norton & Company, Inc.

Library of Congress Cataloging in Publication Data

Sarton, May, 1912-
    The small room.
    (The Norton Library)
    I.   Title.
PZ3.S249Sm5   [PS3537.A832]   813'.5'2   76-25230
ISBN 0-393-00832-0

5 6 7 8 9 0

to DIARMUID RUSSELL

"Teach me to heare Mermaides singing,
Or to keep off envies stinging,
        And finde
        What winde
Serves to advance an honest minde."
                                    John Donne

the small room

Prologue

Lucy Winter sat in the train, swaying and rocking its way north from New York City, with a sense of achievement; the journey set a seal on the depressing limbo of the last months, the stifling summer in New York with her mother; already she sensed the change of air, the lift of autumn. There, out the window, she saw a streak of bright red through a maple. It flashed by like a sign or a symbol, the end of mourning her broken engagement, the actual vivid turn of a leaf toward her first teaching job.

Suddenly, by some trick of light, she was confronted by her own face, standing out enormous against a white farm and rocky pasture, as if a stranger had loomed up out of the New England landscape to stare at her. Was this stern character anyone she knew? She stared back, unsmiling, and judged what she saw: clear wide-apart gray eyes, a large rounded brow, mouth much too thin, soft brown hair held back in a loose knot. I look every inch a female professor, she thought with distaste. What had she got herself into? What indeed? She who had decided to do graduate work at Harvard, quite simply because John would be at the Medical School near by, she who had treated the Doctor's degree as a kind of private joke? No one could have been more serious, and at the same time less so . . . for she considered herself professionally out of the running, but she had loved the work itself. "This has been fun," she said after the oral examination on her thesis. Dr. Winter indeed! Well, here she was, hoist with her own petard, on her way to Appleton of all places—the pristine well, the essence of female institutions of learning! How ironic can life get?

Fortunately she had been much too depressed when she had been interviewed for the job to consider the irony amusing; she had been properly serious. Also she had liked Miss Summerson, had liked her candid blue eyes, her shingled gray head with its aura of the twenties, her air of innocent enthusiasm that made it clear that Lucy would be entering an atmosphere rather different from laissez-faire sophisticated Harvard's. She had been asked searching questions. "You are not planning to marry in the immediate future?"

"I have just broken my engagement."

"Oh, too bad."

At the time Lucy had not found Miss Summerson's obvious relief amusing, but she did now. Then she had been raw, a monster of suffering and self-hatred. She had gone home, she remembered, and told her mother that she was about to be incarcerated, perhaps even for life, since the possibility of tenure in a year or so had been just hinted at. "We are rather a close community and the personal element counts. Whether you are happy with us, and how you get on the first year will show us the way."

Lucy had repressed a smile; it did sound rather like a novitiate. Would she find she had a true vocation? Did she belong in this peculiar order?

Here in the train, on her way out of the tunnel of suffering and self-analysis, she could ask the question with a tremor of excitement. Her face had disappeared from the window, and she looked out at the villages with delight, the ancient brick factories, the white steeples, the differing arrangements of clapboard houses, chimneys, and lilac bushes. There was something peculiarly satisfying to her mind about the New England scene, the austerity and—yes —the elegance of it, she thought, as the train rushed past an open field with a single wine-glass elm standing alone among the goldenrod, a solitary splendor, a green fountain. Whatever Appleton might turn out to be, at least it was rooted in a landscape she found moving beyond her power to analyse. Her father had come from one of these little towns, perhaps that was partly why it felt like home, more than the big old-fashioned apartment on New York's West side where she had herself grown up, and where she had suffered from being the only child of a man too absorbed in his own work to be a father. It was perhaps significant that the long obituary in the *Times* had failed (through some negligence) to mention his family, as if indeed she and her mother had been irrelevant to the implacable inner line, the endless search for more delicate methods in performing surgical operations on the heart. There had been hours lately when she had begun to miss acutely the father she never had; at the time of his death her love affair with John had shut out grief, had immunized her. Now that too was finished, she felt doubly deprived . . . now she had said goodbye to her obsessive passionate war with him, would she at last come to terms with her father? She held twenty-seven years of life in her hands. What would become of it? Of what use would it be?

CHAPTER 1

Lucy was glad to leave her dreary room at the Faculty Club, leave the half-unpacked boxes of books and clothes, leave the ugly maple desk, and make her way across the campus to Hallie Summerson's for tea. At first glance the college bore little resemblance to her romantic image of what it might have been; there was only one beautiful building, Palladian white pillars and the echo of Greece in the pediment; it went back to the days of the seminary, had once been a church, and was now the library. The chapel was Gothic; stained-glass angels carried lilies in their hands, memorializing a student who died young. Most of the other buildings were a mortifying red brick with ugly slate roofs and narrow windows. But, as Lucy walked across the campus in the afternoon light, she

saw that the anomalous collection of buildings was re-
deemed by the trees that wove their rich garlands, their
splendid fountains and rococo arches in and out among the
boring rectangular spaces, and gave the whole scene a kind
of grace. She recognized Hallie Summerson's house in the
distance—white, black, shutters, Gothic windows, so it had
been described. To Lucy, in her unnerved state, it looked
like a house in a fairy tale by Grimm, the scene of some
dreadful confrontation. Would Carryl Cope be there, she
wondered? Miss Summerson had murmured that she might
be, and the murmur had been reverent. Appleton was a
small enough college so that its stars burned with a peculiar ferocity. "Tiger, tiger, burning bright" . . . Miss Cope's
reputation was of that brilliance, that magnitude. One had
heard of her even if one's own subject was American literature and hers mediaeval history. She transcended her subject and the college. Odd that she had not chosen to teach
in a university where she would have dealt with graduate
students. As Lucy walked up the path, she wondered why;
as she rang the bell, trembling absurdly, she remembered
that Professor Cope was always dashing off on leave of
absence to study Arabic or drive a jeep around Turkey exploring crusader castles—no doubt the powers at Appleton
were indulgent to such excursions from academic routine.

The opening door interrupted these thoughts. Hallie
Summerson welcomed her warmly, drew her into the par-
lor with one hand, and waved at a young couple with the
other. "Here's Miss Winter, American literature. Mr. Atwood is doing his dissertation on Fielding. Do sit down, all

of you!" She gestured vaguely at the various chairs, the small worn sofa, and disappeared into the kitchen.

The room, warmed by the September sunlight, was delightfully Victorian without self-consciousness; there were a few etchings and prints of cathedrals on the walls, and a death mask of Keats on the mantel. It felt like a room where thoughts could be spoken with ease, a room that could absorb shock.

"I feel awfully shy, don't you?" Lucy turned to Henry Atwood, sandy-haired, pink, who had been cracking his knuckles.

"Henry feels like a small cock in a yard of huge hens," his wife answered for him. In knee-length socks, a blazer, and a pleated skirt, she looked absurdly young.

"It is rather a female institution, one gathers."

"At least it's near Widener," Henry explained, with a hunted smile. "We've been miles from a good library these years, and I do need books."

The doorbell gave a loud peal, and since Miss Summerson did not appear, Lucy thought she had better answer its imperative summons.

"My name's Cope. Who are you?" Miss Cope uttered in one breath, just as Harriet Summerson dashed in with a tea pot in one hand and a hot water jug in the other.

"Come in, Carryl. This is Miss Winter, and Henry and Deborah Atwood, the new members of the department."

Lucy had expected Carryl Cope to be huge (after all she was a monument, so to speak, already), and she was quite small. She had expected her to be handsome, and saw instead a faded yellowish face, fine hair like a child's, cut short, no make-up at all, eyes that narrowed rather than opened so one could not name their color, and a very pointed nose. She wore a crumpled seersucker suit and had, Lucy noted, small feet in elegant black slippers like a man's evening slippers.

"Sit down, you people!" Miss Summerson admonished them. "I just have to butter the muffins. Oh dear, there's the bell! Carryl, do go . . . I'll be back in half a second. . . ."

It was Professor Beveridge and his wife (Beveridge, Lucy seemed to remember, was Romance languages), and a Miss Finch whom Lucy could not place. Gentle and tentative, a braid of hair coiled round her head, she gravitated toward Carryl Cope. Maria Beveridge stood in the middle of the room like some huge plant from another zone; amply built, dark hair caught back in a barrette, dark eyes heavily shadowed, a wide bright mouth, a black dress —she was inescapably "foreign," and Lucy was so absorbed in trying to decide Italian or Spanish, or what, that she hardly noticed Professor Beveridge himself until she realized that he had addressed her.

"I'm sorry. Did you ask me something?"

She saw that he was thin, tall, and faintly withered; his eyes were pale blue; the life of the face was gathered in their quick intense glance. Below them, the mouth drew itself down in a nervous tic, which Lucy did not find repellent.

"Oh," she answered the repeated question, "yes, I'm terribly new here. It's my first day."

"We'll temper the wind," he said gravely.

"Is there a wind?" she asked, responding to the twinkle in his eye.

"Damn nonsense!" Carryl Cope's voice reached them from the embrasure of the window where she and Miss Finch had taken refuge. "Hallie!" she cried imperiously, "Where are you?"

"Coming," Hallie Summerson appeared in the doorway, bearing a plate of English muffins. "You may well say, 'at last'! You see, I burned the first batch. Do sit down, all of you."

"What is all this I hear about appointing a resident psychiatrist? Jennifer has just been telling me about it. Those psychologists, I suppose. At it again!" Carryl Cope stood with her back to the fire and dominated the room, while she accepted the first cup of tea and drank it down in one gulp.

"Well, after all, 'it' is their business, isn't it?" Hallie answered, unruffled. "But we are not going to talk shop, Carryl." Lucy was amused at her firmness. "Have a muffin."

"Oh? What are we going to talk about then? The price of putty?"

"I understand it is very expensive," Jack Beveridge said.

There was a rippling smile. There was a pause. The room now seemed crowded, and when they did find chairs,

Deborah Atwood chose the floor, where she looked more like an undergraduate than ever.

"Who is this child?" Miss Cope looked down at her with an air of unbelief.

"Deborah Atwood," the child answered for herself.

"Are you to teach?"

"No, my husband—Henry is."

"Oh, Mr. Atwood, assistant professor, of course." And Carryl Cope turned to discover him, with obvious relief.

"I wish you would sit down, Carryl," Harriet Summerson said.

"I like standing."

"You tower enough as it is."

"Don't be rude, Hallie. We have to impress these new professors."

"Shall we give them the treatment?" Jack Beveridge asked from the far corner where he was sitting on a stool, his cup balanced precariously on his knee. "Or shall we just gently torture them a little while?"

"Do we have to be initiated?" Deborah asked demurely. "Is Appleton a secret society?"

"Of course it is. Every college is."

The conversation seemed to Lucy so mannered and unreal that she felt incapable of uttering a word. It was as if everyone, except possibly Harriet Summerson, were playing a role, and she suspected that even Hallie Summerson's brusque naturalness might be a mask, a slightly subtler mask than those the others had chosen to wear.

"Tell us a little about this secret society then." Henry

Atwood looked, Lucy thought, wonderfully happy, as if he had arrived at some long-hoped-for destination. This was endearing.

"But we know nothing about it ourselves," Carryl Cope said with a relentless smile. "You are the anthropologists confronting a strange tribe."

"Not so much a tribe as a personality." Miss Finch stretched her knotted fingers toward the fire. "I do agree that first impressions may be more valid than what one thinks one knows later, more objective; there is an atmosphere, of course, a very specific atmosphere . . ."

"And just what is it, Jennifer?" Jack Beveridge interrupted. "Define it for us, do!"

Lucy noted that although Jennifer Finch, brown and mousy, appeared to be the least assuming person in the room, they turned to her with deference, a deference different from the playful obeisances directed toward Carryl Cope.

Miss Finch did not leap into the conversation with the speed of light as the others did. She alone, perhaps, was not playing a part, took no stance, but was simply thinking aloud in the presence of friends. "Let me put some apparently unrelated things together. You have noticed our Palladian library?"

"Yes indeed," Lucy responded instantly. "It's beautiful."

"Those white pillars that look so well in the snow— yes—" she proceeded as delicately as a water beetle skating the surface of a pool—"and let us not forget that Miss Cecilia Wellington founded the college on her father's money, after his death, because he had refused to allow her to go to Radcliffe (then known as The Annex, you remember); she went to Oxford instead, when she was nearly fifty, a late and, we must believe, not unfruitful revenge upon Papa; there is also the fact that Appleton, unlike most of the colleges founded in that period, is not and never has been affiliated with a church; the sciences, notably mathematics, have been more emphasized here than is usual in women's colleges. An atmosphere?" she queried. "Very hard to pin down, but I think I am not being unduly chauvinistic if I say that there is still a certain edge, an edge of excitement in being admitted to Appleton."

"The last stronghold of the bluestocking, perhaps?" Jack Beveridge inserted slyly.

"And why not?" Carryl Cope fired back at once. "We don't teach domestic science; we are not interested especially in producing marriageable young ladies."

"They do seem to have exceptionally bad manners," Jack murmured.

Carryl Cope did not hear this remark; she had turned to Jennifer with unexpected gentleness and said, "We interrupted you. Do go on."

"We have tended to foster the brilliant student." Miss Finch swallowed a smile with a delightful air of internal amusement. "Odd that this should set us apart. One would have supposed the fostering of brilliance to be the function of a college."

"But what becomes of them afterwards?" Lucy innocently asked. "I mean, is this a society in which brilliance in women is considered desirable?"

The three women professors answered volubly at once.

"The college was not founded to give society what it wants," she heard Miss Cope, sharp and glittering. "Quite the contrary!"

But it was Harriet Summerson's voice which finally rose above the others. She was quite flushed, Lucy noticed, but whether this was a response to the question or caused by the exigencies of the tea table, it was hard to tell. Her remarks were punctuated by her lifting the tea pot and waving it, first at one and then at another of her guests, while Henry Atwood carried cups to and fro. "I don't think brilliance is quite the right word, Jennifer. We have presumed that by setting an uncompromising standard we might develop women who could take the lead, who would become responsible in the deepest sense. Shoddy work, students who manage to 'get by,' are not going to grow into mature people, capable of handling power. We prize excellence."

"I'm getting more and more nervous about my first class," Lucy said mischievously.

"The freshmen do not yet know about excellence," Jack Beveridge said. "I doubt if you need to worry."

"The fact is," Jennifer Finch continued her monologue, so often interrupted in the last few minutes, "that to maintain anything remotely resembling scholarship, one has to talk as if Appleton were a sort of nunnery where only the dedicated come to breathe a rarefied air. Possibly we achieve a slight degree of scholastic superiority by these heroic attitudes; sometimes we are merely ridiculous," she ended, curiously remote, curiously detached.

The animation of a few moments before had subsided. Carryl Cope tapped a cigarette on her tortoise shell case.

"I wonder what really happens?" Among the other voices, Maria's had a curious lilt, not an accent so much as the expression of a temperament several degrees warmer than that of anyone who had spoken so far. "Young girls are like chameleons; they take on the color of their surroundings. Perhaps your bluestockings are just red or black stockings in disguise: put them in a school of domestic science and they will bake pies with just the awe they bring to Greek now. Are they moulded or do they achieve merely a perfection of imitation, learn to please their present masters? That Seaman girl, for instance. What is she really like?"

"Jane Seaman is a scholar. I'll vouch for that," Carryl said. "That girl will go far."

"Where will she go?" Maria pressed her point.

"She'll do original work."

"Is she hungry and thirsty?" Maria asked. "She strikes me as rather smug." There was, Lucy sensed, tension between these two women, as different as night and day.

"And why not, pray? She's head and shoulders above anyone else in the senior class, intellectually speaking, and she's worked like a demon."

"No shop talk," Harriet Summerson interrupted. "After

all, the Atwoods and Miss Winter don't even know who Jane Seaman is."

"Oh, do go on! I find it fascinating," Lucy said.

"As a matter of fact, Jane has registered for your American Renaissance course, so you'll meet her soon enough."

"Oh dear." Lucy's dismay turned to embarrassment when everyone laughed.

"Actually," Jack Beveridge said, "Jane is rather fun." Jack provided some essence that was welcome among the intensities, the elaborate self-defence of the women professors. He provided the salt; also, Lucy felt he was kind.

"You can't imagine the relief it is to be here." Henry Atwood burst into speech as a bird might burst into song, so great was his pleasure in the occasion and in himself for being present. "At Appleton, I mean." He turned to his wife, who was helping to collect cups and saucers. "Isn't it, Debby? You see, where we were—"

"Where were you?" Carryl Cope asked.

"A little college in northern Michigan, Defoe. I'm sure you've never heard of it. Anyway, all they talked about there was religion and sports."

"And whether anyone had been caught smoking," Debby chimed in.

"Smoking, of course, was a sin." His round face beamed. "Probably brilliance in a woman would also have been thought a sin, but there was no opportunity to discover."

"It does sound peculiarly grim," Carryl Cope said distantly. She was visibly not interested in what went on in northern Michigan.

"Didn't it make you feel like awful snobs?" Maria asked. Deborah shot her a quick startled glance. "Did you stop smoking, or did you smoke ostentatiously to prove your integrity?"

Henry blinked and swallowed. It was clear that he thought he had caught the tone of the occasion and now feared he had missed a cue. "We were very uncomfortable," he said humbly. Lucy had not expected such transparent ingenuousness in a colleague; he is a dear, she thought. "I hated it, as a matter of fact. I hated feeling superior. I felt I was everything they dislike about the East. I'm sure we failed somehow."

"No," Debby was vehement. "You had two good students and one of them will go on to Chicago. That's not failure."

"You make us feel overprotected," Harriet Summerson said.

"Against ignorance and sloth, why not?" The tiger showed its claws for the first time. You had to be a little inhuman, Lucy suspected, to be as secure as Carryl Cope.

"It's time I got home to Mother." The remark seemed incongruous coming from Jennifer Finch, who rose from her chair to make it. Lucy had imagined her as living alone with a cat. Now in the general movement of departure the front door stood open into the late afternoon sunlight, and there was the casual feel of a summer evening, of time opening out. Children went by on bicycles ringing their bells. Lucy, the last to say goodbye, asked if she could help wash up.

"Well, that's very kind of you, Dr. Winter."

"Do call me Lucy, please."

"Very well, Lucy, come along to the kitchen. It will only take a moment, and we can go on talking. I always hate it when everyone leaves at once, don't you? One is left high and dry."

There was an old-fashioned wood-burning stove in one corner, covered with newspapers and used as a general dump. The window sills had rows of plants in odd jars along them, geraniums mostly. The linoleum was worn; in the center of the room stood a deal table, its clean wood scrubbed. They washed the dishes at a soapstone sink. "I do like your kitchen," Lucy said, standing with a towel in her hand, ready to wipe.

"It's awfully old-fashioned. But I know where everything is and can put my hands on it without opening and shutting a lot of little doors." Harriet Summerson worked quickly but absent-mindedly. At this moment she dumped the full sugar bowl into the dishpan. "Good Lord, what have I done now?" She burst into laughter, Lucy laughed too, and felt suddenly at home.

"I'm going to like it here," she said, watching Miss Summerson pour the whole dishpan of water and sugar out, and rescue the cups and saucers. "I liked all those people."

"It's a kind of zoo, really. I sometimes think we collect every species, but they *are* wonderful people. It may be a safe little world, but it's an immensely alive one. You will not be bored."

"Does Maria Beveridge teach?"

"She used to. Jack met her at Middlebury. But now they have three little boys, you see."

"How lovely to have three little boys!"

"Don't underestimate Jack, by the way. He's first class. He's developed an attitude of irony, cynicism, whatever it is, but that's only a defence—hard to be a man in this female seminary." She had become brusque with shyness. "I like Maria. She has the effect of a quiet storm, or perhaps I should say a quieting storm: she clears the air."

"Yes," Lucy said. "I can see that. She's quite formidable."

"High voltage all right, but on a different current from most of us. She's not really an intellectual. She's a nature. That's why she disturbs Carryl."

Lucy smiled. "I shouldn't have thought anything could disturb Carryl Cope."

"Lots of things do." Harriet Summerson put the last cup into the drainer with an air of finality. She did not explain herself and Lucy didn't dare ask. It was clearly time to leave.

Miss Summerson turned and, leaning her back against the sink, pushed back her hair. Her eyes were as blue as a summer sea. "The hell of teaching is that one is never prepared. I often think that before every class I feel the same sort of terror I used to experience before an examination . . . and always I imagine that next year it will be different." Lucy sensed that here, standing in the kitchen, she was close to the pulse of the life she was about to enter. She was in the presence of a mystery. It was not the words, ordinary enough, nor even what they expressed, but something intangible about Harriet Summerson herself, who now stood up and said, "I would like to ask you to stay for supper . . . that's what all this has been about . . . but I must work."

"So must I," Lucy said fervently.

At the door they shook hands. Then Harriet Summerson looked off into the long bands of sunlight lying across the road. "Is there a life more riddled with self-doubt than that of a woman professor, I wonder?" she asked the evening air.

Lucy walked back across the campus with Harriet Summerson's question reverberating in her mind, and looked at the ugly red buildings with new eyes. She realized that the parting from John and its resonance had insulated her until now from thinking very much about the sort of life she was poised to enter, what joys and perils, what anxieties and power to endure lay ahead. Of course the absence of students had something to do with it; the most important element in this world was still lacking. Tomorrow and for all the days following it for a long autumn, winter, and spring, her attention would be focussed on a bevy of girls whom she could not even imagine. Would she be able to swing it? What could she tell them? What did she really know?

CHAPTER 2

The girls arrived, and settled like flocks of garrulous starlings, perpetual chatter and perpetual motion. Lucy, looking down from her office on the fourth floor of one of the oldest buildings, compared the campus to a stage where a complicated ballet was being rehearsed. Small groups flowed together and parted; a girl in a blue blazer ran from one building to another; five or six others arranged themselves under an elm, in unconsciously romantic attitudes, a chorus of nymphs. The effect was enhanced by the freshmen's required red Eton caps, and by the unrequired but almost universal uniform of short pleated skirts and blazers. Looking down on all this casual, yet intimate life from above, Lucy felt lonely and a little scared.

If she had feared that Appleton's emphasis on scholarship might have brought forth a group of cranks or creeps, girls in spectacles, girls who walk with their heads down, monsters of morose self-absorption and shyness, the reverse appeared to be true. They were frighteningly healthy and natural, but undifferentiated. And Lucy longed to separate the dancing corps into individual faces and names, to make contact with an actual class. She sighed and turned back to her desk, threw out the notes she had been laboriously making, and decided suddenly to do something quite different. To prepare for this first class, she found herself exploring and recovering areas in herself that had been blotted out by the last years. She had been living in someone else, now she must draw on herself. She had never realized until now what extraordinary teachers she had had, nor what complex threads had been woven together to bring her to the moment, this perilous, exhilarating moment when she would be asked to summon all that she held in her hands and to communicate it.

At precisely five minutes past the hour a few days later she walked into Holmes D, to meet the American Renaissance section. The dinginess of the room struck her between the eyes, and also the unfocussed look of the twelve or so girls scattered about it. Her knees trembled idiotically as she stepped onto the small platform and sat down behind the desk. She looked up, met a pair of rather vague blue eyes, and dropped hers. The moment was of a gravity for her, had a weight that it could not possibly have for them, after all. They had not approached this hour with their hearts skipping a beat, with a prickle of gooseflesh on their skins. In the second's pause, panic flowed in. She held it at bay by asking them in a rather firm voice to tell her their names. While they did so, she looked at the faces, a mistake, for, when they had all spoken, she realized that she had attached only one name to a person, that of Jane Seaman. The prize student sat hunched over, fair hair falling over one eye, a small-featured, secretive face that yielded nothing of itself. Lucy was conscious of being rather sardonically observed, and responded by stating at once that this was not going to be an easy course, that it would require extensive reading, and two major papers.

"I am not going to lecture after today," she said, "I shall expect you to do the talking, and in fact we shall consider ourselves a seminar." She felt rising in her a faint intoxication, stemming from the concentrated attention that faced her. With it came a wave of happiness. What will *she* think of Thoreau, she asked herself, her eyes resting on a girl with a curiously old-fashioned look. Her face formed a perfect oval; she had reddish curly hair; her eyes seemed very wide-open or on the verge of tears (odd)—was her name Pippa? Lucy tried vainly to remember, as she opened her notebook and took a deep breath. This was it.

"It occurred to me that a lively class—and I hope you will prove to be that—is rather like a tennis match. If so, you have a right to know something about your opponent on the court. So I am taking the period today to tell you where I stand. It will give you a clue to prejudices and predilections, as well as a clue to beliefs and standards."

Lucy sensed the increased stir of attention; those who had brought books closed them with an air of expectation.

"As I thought about meeting you today, I looked back over my own education and was astonished at how rich and complex, how various the attitudes had been, and how various the demands made upon me by the great teachers in my life, how massive their influence."

There was a pause. Lucy felt compelled to get up, walk down from the raised platform to the windows, and look out, as she talked to them first about her father. "His hobby," she said, "was cabinet-making. In the large old-fashioned apartment where we lived one room was devoted to his tools and workbench." How dull it sounded! She longed to make this room vivid, to evoke in the dank classroom its sweet clean smells of wax, of resin and turpentine. She longed to bring before them her father in an old pair of dungarees, the look of happy concentration on his face as he whistled Gilbert and Sullivan tunes, the way his delicate surgeon's hand stroked a piece of wood. What she could not tell them, but it swept over her in a wave of poignant regret, was how as a child she had longed for the same care and tenderness toward herself. Had she been silent for long? She was suddenly acutely aware of the loud tick of the clock on the wall, jerking the minutes away, admonishing her to keep to the subject. She spoke brusquely now, in an accelerated tempo, of what she had learned from her father about the importance of slow careful work, of close attention to detail, and of how much she had, as a child, resented his compulsive neatness. "You will discover," she added with a smile, "that you appreciate teachers rather a long time after you have suffered from them."

Her smile was answered with a ripple of response. She was discovering that she could talk to these girls with perfect directness, in a way she had never been able to talk to anyone before in her life, as if the group of twelve were itself an entity, a delightfully giving personality, and as if she—freed by the strangely intimate yet impersonal circumstance—could give it something of herself that she would never be able to give to an individual human being.

She spoke then of a woman teacher whose rages had taught the terrified students a respect for France and French civilization that had lasted through their lives. "It is hard for me even now," Lucy heard herself saying, "to detach myself from the conviction I held at twelve years old that the French are superior in every way to everyone else." (Dear Mademoiselle Monnet she thought, as she sat down to look at her notes, where are you now? With your elegance and fury, with your radiant joy as you recited La Fontaine?) "We learned to respect a subject—in a school where it seemed often that we ourselves were the main subject of passionate attention."

The irony in Lucy's tone escaped her listeners, she felt, but if she had lost them briefly, they came back as she spoke of Mr. Nagle who had given up a highly-paid job on *Life* magazine because he wanted to teach English. What a sacred phenomenon he had appeared to his students, many of whose parents would have thought such a decision simply crazy! "But that was not why he was a great teacher," she reminded them and herself. "I have come to see that he communicated to us a rather rare quality in my profession." Lucy was so startled to hear herself use the phrase "my profession" that she stammered slightly as if she had just told a lie. "It w-w-was humility. He was devastatingly honest, with a kind of honesty that forced him to ask questions rather than to make statements, and to question himself as seriously as he did us."

Jane Seaman was looking out the window. Bored? It was possible, after all, that the whole idea of this lecture was a fiasco, and they were finding her merely absurd. The clock gave another loud tick, as the hand jerked away another minute. Yet, in the tension established in her own mind *vis à vis* Jane Seaman, Lucy found strength. I'll make her pay attention, she said to herself, launching into a description of the professor of philosophy she had sat under in college. She explained that she had failed the midyear examination in Professor Greene's course, but that he had taken the trouble to call her in and talk it over, although this was a class of two hundred and such attentions were hardly to be expected.

"'You're trying to jump the gun, Miss . . .' and I remember he had to look for my name on the blue book . . . He told me that my paper was clumsy, but that it contained one original concept. Was I aware of that? [I was not.] Well, I had better hold my horses and master the subject before I launched into private speculations. 'However,' he added with a severely uncompromising look in his eye, 'I respect you, Miss Winter, and you must learn to respect yourself. The people who made A on this exam may never think an original thought. You can. You'll do better next time, please.' Well," Lucy smiled, "you can imagine how hard I worked after that!"

She noticed then, at what had seemed a moment of triumph, that the girls were gathering their books together, and there was a faint stirring among them as of a flock of birds about to rise and fly away. She still had five minutes, and she swung out into the air like a trapeze artist, forcing their attention back by the recklessness of her drive.

"I have just one more exemplar and the record will be complete. Professor Hardy, in my own field of American literature, was a tease—genial, outgoing, the kind of professor who actually seems to enjoy having students around. He said that the trouble with women students" (immediately Lucy felt the prickle of renewed attention) "is that their very intensity gets in the way of the valuable nonchalant roving eye. I'm sure you have realized at the end of this hour of self-revelation that I am one of the serious characters to whom these remarks were addressed. Professor Hardy opened out for all of us the conception of what the French used to call the 'gai scavoir.' You are not yet aware of the excruciating self-tortures Ph.D. students go through, nor how remarkable this professor was, who wore his learning so lightly that he forced you to wear yours with at least an attempt at a sense of proportion. I'm afraid that most of us were rather more like elephants dancing than like Ariel," (was Jane Seaman smiling? Lucy thought she caught a fleeting smile on that ungiving face) "but we could imagine the lightness mastery makes possible. I shall try not to take you too seriously, and I hope that sentiment may be reciprocated." Lucy glanced nervously at the clock and added, "Whew! I just managed to get in under the line!" The bell pealed out like some dreadful siren, and at once the whole building trembled as classes tumbled out and thundered down the stairs. "Until next week and Mr. Thoreau!"

Lucy closed her notebook, got up, and was about to make her escape when she was stopped at the door by the Victorian-looking redhead she had noticed early in the hour. The others eddied round them.

"That was very interesting, Miss Winter. Especially about your father."

"Thank you," Lucy said. She did not want to speak to anyone at the moment. "What is your name? I must begin to try to remember names . . ."

"Pippa Brentwood."

They stood there. Pippa hesitated on the brink of whatever it was she wished to say. She blushed. Tears, to Lucy's horror, sprang to her eyes. "About your father . . . You see, my father died this summer."

After all, Lucy had chosen to speak to them first on a

personal level. But this intimacy upset her. She wanted to continue to speak to the class as an entity; her instinct was to shy away. She fumbled with her purse and wondered how on earth to handle this plea for sympathy, for pity, for understanding from a perfect stranger.

"Oh, I'm sorry," she murmured. "That is hard. Are you a Senior?"

"Yes."

They were stranded there in the empty classroom, while the roar of life went on around them.

"Thank you for telling me," Lucy said because she could not summon any other remark that would not bring forth, she sensed, a flood of tears. "Well, I'll see you next week," and, abruptly, she fled.

Self-doubt, Harriet Summerson had said; Lucy blushed inwardly the whole way across the campus to meet her for lunch at the faculty club. The superficiality of what she herself had managed to utter in the last hour appalled her. Exactitude, commitment, humility, self-respect indeed! She had even forgotten to sum up in those four words what she had meant to get over to the class.

But, in the midst of this bitter self-examination, it was a relief to sit down opposite Hallie Summerson. Today in a blue tweed suit with a liberty silk print of small blue flowers beneath it, she was aesthetically satisfying, because so completely what she was; no vestige of make-up concealed the fine lines round her clear blue eyes. They sat where they could look out on the lawn, already dotted with scarlet and yellow maple leaves.

When they had ordered creamed chicken, ice cream and coffee—nursery food, Lucy thought, perfectly suited to her shaken state of mind—and when they had talked about autumn and how lovely it could be in New England, Hallie paused and shot Lucy an observant glance. "Well, how did it go? I've already heard one report, so you see I am not afraid to ask the question."

"It was an experiment" (but what exactly had Miss Summerson heard?) "and at the moment I can only think that it failed."

"Good sign," Miss Summerson nodded. "One always gets a negative reaction after a good class. It's one of the hazards of the profession."

"Is it?"

"You've given a piece of yourself away, even if it is only a certain amount of nervous energy, don't you know? And you are a bit deflated as a result—diminished, one might say."

"Oh." Lucy considered this and rejected it. "What depressed me, I think, was that I tried to say something about learning and teaching, and the only result was that a girl wanted to tell me about her father's death."

"Pippa Brentwood, I expect. She does tend to dramatize," Hallie answered Lucy's nod, "and I'm afraid her father's death, sudden and tragic as it was, has given her rather a chance to indulge herself."

"I felt cornered. I don't believe in personal relationships between teachers and students, do you?"

Miss Summerson raised her eyebrows with an air of faint amusement. "Theoretically, no."

"But it happens that the theory doesn't work?"

"Maybe you are one of the rare professors in a college of this sort who can keep her distance. That would be wisdom."

"Rare in one so young?" Lucy responded to the ironic tone.

"Rare."

"No comment," Lucy laughed. It was a relief to be talking to an adult for a change. "It's amazing how after just one class, I realize things I hadn't even imagined."

"For instance?"

"For instance, the rather suspect intoxication of the captive audience. These girls are almost uncannily responsive."

"They can be almost uncannily *un*responsive too," and Hallie seemed lit up from inside with amusement. When she spoke again, it was on a different level from the chaffing tone she had used until now. She was suddenly serious. "I'm going back to what you said about personal relationships. One of the problems is simply that after a month of watching you and listening to you in class, your students know you far better and more intimately than you will ever know them. They feel related to you, you see."

"Oh dear, yes, I do see," Lucy said, the quaking she had experienced just after the class returning in full force.

"Part of the art of teaching, I have come to believe,

lies in how this pseudo-intimacy is handled. It can be fruitful. Carryl Cope, for instance, is a case in point. Every student of hers is a conquest."

"One senses that. She expects disciples."

"Don't be censorious too quickly," Harriet Summerson said a shade impatiently. "You see, girls will respond to feeling always; what is hard is to get them to *think*. Carryl may have disciples, but they do not become so without learning a great deal about mediaeval history, a great deal more than they will ever know about Carryl."

"Jane Seaman is one of those, I take it."

"Jane is Carryl's exhibit Number One at the moment. And Jane was a pretty rough diamond when she arrived —rich, spoiled, arrogant. She has learned to think and to work hard."

"But perhaps not to be humble?" Lucy could not resist.

Had she gone too far? At this second, Harriet Summerson visibly withdrew. Loyalty to a friend and colleague? At any rate, she changed the subject.

"It might interest you, before you get smothered in freshman papers, to look in on one of Jennifer Finch's classes." The gently chaffing tone had returned. "She carries out your theories."

"Yes," Lucy responded at once. "At your tea she dominated, yet she seemed at first the most unassuming person there. I was fascinated."

"Visit a class . . ." Miss Summerson held out the prospect rather like a carrot to a donkey, Lucy felt.

"Miss Finch said something about having to go home to her mother. It was a little startling."

"Oh yes, she's the classic old-maid professor, bound hand and foot to an autocrat. We have all prayed for Mrs. Finch's demise, without avail. She has an iron constitution, of course."

"And Miss Finch has not been limited by—" Lucy hunted for a word and did not find one.

She caught the twinkle in Miss Summerson's candid eye. "We are all limited by something or other. Thank God for transcendance, sublimation, and all those other dirty words, say I, all those suspect ways of handling impossible circumstances or one's own impossible self!" When she spoke out like this, Miss Summerson's whole face went pink.

"Yes," Lucy sighed, remembering her violent arguments with John on this subject. "We've become dreadfully self-conscious. That, too, is a limitation, perhaps."

"And just there is Carryl's strength. She simply will not be bothered. You heard her furious reaction to the idea of a committee on mental health? She and her old friend Olive Hunt, who is unfortunately a trustee, have managed to keep the college back in that respect. We are old-fashioned."

"But can one refuse knowledge when it is available?"

"You and I could not. Carryl can. She is, don't forget, one generation ahead of mine, and two ahead of yours, and one cannot wholly transcend one's generation, I fear. Has it ever occurred to you that there is a lag? A generation of young professors emerges who have been formed by the generation preceding them? One of my best professors at Smith was still a Meredith fan because Meredith was avant-garde when she was young. When I began to teach, Joyce, Proust and Virginia Woolf were the great figures: in college we passed around the banned edition of *Ulysses!* How old-fashioned can you get?" Miss Summerson drank a last swallow of coffee and looked at her watch. "Goodness, I almost forgot to tell you what the student I met after your class had to say. It was succinct: 'Miss Winter's neat!'"

Lucy laughed with relief.

"I might add, so you get the full flavor of the word, that this girl was in Europe last summer and told me she had found Chartres 'neat.'"

By the time they said goodbye on the terrace Miss Summerson had suggested that she be called "Hallie," and Lucy felt decidedly restored. It was a good solid feeling to have Hallie Summerson at your back.

CHAPTER 3

The momentum of the
fall semester gathered itself
after that first day and Lucy did not see Hallie Summerson or anyone else among her colleagues for more than
a week. She had imagined that she knew the material
on Thoreau and Emerson almost by heart, that preparation for these first lectures would be easy, but she soon
discovered that knowing something and teaching it are
as different as dreaming and waking. Things she had
never noticed before sprang up at her out of the text;
questions pounced upon her from the class, and the familiar words and ideas startled her as if she had not spent
hours already examining them. She met a surprising
resistance to Thoreau and it unnerved her; the students
were not delighted by his pungent style (style did not

touch them yet) and were irritated by what they called his lack of responsibility and childishness; Jane Seaman defined him as a nineteenth-century beatnik. Lucy found herself getting hot with irritation and bafflement. She felt like a lawyer arguing a case before a hard-hearted jury, and was limp at the end of the hour; three of the girls walked back to the club with her, carrying on the discussion where it had left off when the bell rang. In those ten minutes Lucy had a vivid sense of what the dialogue between pupil and teacher can be at its best. And in the course of it, she understood what it was that made a professor like Carryl Cope respect a student like Jane Seaman. For Jane led the group of anti-Thoreauvians and in doing so kept Lucy on her mettle. This was exhausting but exhilarating, quite different from one of the freshman sections which seemed like a huge passive elephant she had to try to lift each morning. At times Lucy felt desperation, as if she would never catch up, never be really prepared for the next day, or that her head would burst with the sustained hours of concentration she must ask of herself. She marvelled at how much vitality was required: how could people like Hallie Summerson, Carryl Cope, Jack Beveridge keep this up for years and years, lift one elephant after another on sheer gusto and nerve?

Suddenly one day the maples on the campus and on the surrounding hillsides turned; it was a brilliant gold air splashed with vermilion and scarlet, but mostly radiant gold, such a glory of light under the flat blue sky that

Lucy realized for the first time the fact that autumn in New England is something more than a season, some great adventure. But she could not take time out to explore, as she longed to do, because this was the period of freshman conferences. Lucy saw four or five students, each for a half hour or more, every day. She had the impression that the faces which turned toward her eagerly in the classroom closed fatally the minute she confronted them in the dingy cubbyhole that was her office. The room was unyielding. It had a dead smell; dankness descended on her when she sat down in the hard armchair before the scratched ugly desk, and waited for a girl to show up. It was irritating, though not unnatural perhaps, that they were so often late. Susy or Jane or Hannah arrived breathless; dumped an armload of books on the floor; feigned surprise when lateness was remarked upon and Lucy brought out a paper from the folder before her, covered with notes and marks, the signs of her own hard labor, and suggested that they get down to work.

But how, she asked herself on these occasions, without ever being able to give an assured answer, did one do that? She might read a passage aloud, a passage where dangling clauses, half sentences, mixed metaphors, clichés all added up to fuzzy thinking. But the girl sitting there, patient and bored, waiting to be "told," had no inkling of this, was astonished to discover how many mistakes one could fall into, looked innocently dismayed. Lucy was sometimes severe. "When you say you worked hard, what exactly did you do? Sit at a desk and doodle for half an hour?" She was distressed to hear her voice, at these moments, take on the tone of an exasperated governess. Sometimes she laughed, remembering the rhyme she had loved as a child, "You naughty kittens, you've lost your mittens!"

Sometimes the response was sullen: "No one understands me, it is hopeless" was written on the closed face. Patiently then Lucy took the paragraph up again word by word and analysed it, but then the danger was that even to herself the problems involved began to sound so complicated that she was dismayed. Halfway through, she could feel the student's attention wandering to the brilliant leaves outside. It did sound dull!

"Do you think you might try to rewrite this paragraph now while you have it all clearly in mind?"

(Look of terror.)

"Well then, if not now, bring it to class tomorrow."

Was this giving in? Should she have forced the issue? She could hear the footsteps running down the hall like an animal released from a cage, free of having to concentrate, free of having to pin the wandering mind down, having learned next to nothing while Lucy herself had been working furiously hard, and felt drained by the effort she had been making. Beside the hard work in the small room, lecturing seemed easy, but Lucy was aware even after the first afternoon that this was where the real teaching would be done. From these endless half hours of attentive prodding and pushing and nurturing, Hallie Summerson and the others had lifted the girls Lucy enjoyed now as Juniors and Seniors, and she felt something like awe at the achievement.

"May I see you for a moment?" Lucy lifted her head at the end of one afternoon that week and saw Pippa Brentwood, of all people she did not want to see, standing in the doorway. While Pippa sat down and explained haltingly that she had in mind for her paper an essay on the uneasy friendship between Thoreau and Emerson, how the two men had defined it, and why they had failed each other—while she talked eloquently of this, Lucy was aware of this girl's curious distinction; a round white collar over a black sweater set off the oval face, the high round forehead framed in soft red curls, the clear eyes that literally brimmed with feeling.

"Well—" Lucy was, in fact, impressed, "—that sounds rather a good idea. You'll have to do a lot of reading in the journals and letters, but I quite envy you that pleasure."

"Yes," Pippa murmured. "You see, I need to work hard this term. It's better for me if I do."

How unfair it was, Lucy thought, to withdraw at once as if a nerve between them had been touched. "Well, then, go ahead." And, quickly, before Pippa would have a chance to submerge them in the personal, the private world of her grief, Lucy added, "I am curious to see how this lively class writes. You are such an articulate group, but," she smiled, "it doesn't necessarily follow that you will write like angels, I fear."

"We are excited by the course." Pippa blushed furiously.

And before Lucy had time to make a response, she plunged in desperately, "Please help me!" Her eyes had filled with tears.

"I know this is a hard year for you, Pippa, but I think the less you dramatize—" How harsh it sounded!

"It's real suffering," Pippa wailed, and the tears poured down her cheeks like summer rain. "You can't say it's not real!"

Face this, Lucy admonished herself. Be kind. After all, she's only a child.

"Of course it's real. The loss of one's father at any age . . ." But where to go from here? "Is your mother finding it very hard?" She heard the tone of her voice, cool, sympathetic, yet withholding. It was hateful to be in this position where it was kindness to appear a little less than human. The question only produced loud sobs. Lucy talked on at random, saying all the commonplaces about death, about time, waiting for the girl to regain command of herself.

"You see," Pippa said after blowing her nose, "I wasn't there. I went away for the weekend, although he asked me to stay . . . it's that." Tears flowed again.

So here it was again the old universal wound, Lucy thought, feeling pity for the first time. She found herself speaking quite gently now about the load of guilt children always do carry around about their parents, and how self-blame can, after a point, become self-indulgence. "It's the human condition, Pippa."

"Is it?" It was touching to see the immense relief in

the face of innocence before her, relief like some clear dawn taking the place of disintegration and darkness. "I knew you'd understand. I knew you'd help."

"But I've done nothing but utter some old saws!"

"It's so wonderful to be able to talk to you at last."

At last, Lucy thought, indeed! The sherry-colored eyes were radiant. "Well," she said briskly, "I'm glad I could help."

"You won't refuse to see me?"

So, here it was and no escaping the necessity to be cold.

"On professional matters, Pippa, I'll always be here. This has been an excursion outside them."

"I'm a terrible nuisance, I guess," Pippa said hopefully.

"No," Lucy summoned dispassion to her side as if it were a guardian angel. "But you are, perhaps, confusing me with someone else, an imaginary someone, let us say, 'a father confessor and friend.' I don't see myself in that role, I'm afraid." Lucy got up and stood with her back to the window. It was meant to be a dismissal.

"You sound so hard," Pippa said in an accusing voice.

"I'm not hard," she shot back, fatally on the defensive. "I'm too vulnerable. I have never been a teacher before. And I don't believe in college teachers being amateur psychoanalysts." She recovered herself firmly. "There must be a subject between us, Pippa, an impersonal subject," she said, facing the girl squarely.

"Well," Pippa, accepting defeat, gathered her books together as slowly as possible, "but if I could just see you when I get desperate? I'll try not to, I really will," she added eagerly.

"I'm not a monster, after all," Lucy said, and left it at that.

Pippa would have been delighted by the chaos she left behind her. Lucy stood at the window a long time, looking down on an already leafless maple, and the wind blowing the dried gold leaves about on the grass. Two girls went by arm in arm. She glanced from them to the white pillars of the library. How cool and discreet the world outside looked compared to the confused, upset, muddled world of this small room where so much happened and did not happen. She had behaved herself, Lucy thought with dismay, like an insufferable prig. Oh, what a bore it was to have to endure those penetrating, innocent, suffering, demanding eyes of Pippa's, those sherry-colored eyes that wept as easily as a summer shower! I want to be free to teach my students in peace, she thought. I want to be free to do that unselfconsciously, without all this personal stuff. I want to be allowed to give what I can give.

But had one any right to protect oneself? What had she been protecting? A relationship that could not be maintained as fruitful if it lapsed into personalities? And what was teaching all about anyway? If one did not believe one was teaching people how to live, how to experience, giving them the means to ripen, then what did one believe? Was it knowledge that concerned her primarily? And would knowledge alone bring them to appreciate Thoreau?

Lucy glanced at her watch and was filled with relief at the thought that she was invited out to dinner at the Beveridges', filled with relief to lay these thoughts and questions aside and hurry to get dressed, and to be a private person for a change.

CHAPTER 4

The Atwoods and—of all people—the President himself, Blake Tillotson, were the other guests.

"Well," he said, as he settled down in a big armchair, "I'm delighted to meet you people!"

A shrewd kindly face, that of a small-town banker, one might have guessed. He had actually been a Unitarian minister, had worked with the Service Committee in Germany after the war, and, Lucy remembered, had written a book about that experience. She disliked "good works," and cared so little about politics that she sometimes failed to vote, so she had not read his book and did not intend to. Also she had sensed the college attitude, which was disdain of the administration in general. Still, Tillotson had done the right thing during the McCarthy business, and had had several terse exchanges with the local American Legion—about Hallie Summerson, no doubt. "We give him a C plus," someone or other had said to Lucy not long ago, on the grounds that he had pretty well failed as a money raiser. He's a nice guy, Lucy thought, even if he won't take a martini. He had turned to Henry to ask how things were going.

"It's a shock to teach students so eager to learn!"

"Women are always eager to learn," Maria was passing a bowl of red caviar and crackers. "This is the great advantage of a female seminary."

"It has all the assets of a nunnery and none of the liabilities, perhaps?" The President was quicker than Lucy had imagined he would be.

"I don't miss the boys," Henry Atwood said, and was astonished at the burst of laughter that greeted his remark.

Lucy let the conversation go on around her, happy to be passive and to make no effort, to look around the room and feel her way into the Beveridges' life here. Where were the little boys? They were nowhere to be seen, though she had noticed a small bicycle in the front hall, and a large sheet of brown paper covered with red and blue lines tacked up on the wall. The Beveridges were modern: white walls, suspended shelves filled with French and Italian books in paper covers, no reproductions of Impressionist painters, she noted with satisfaction. The furniture was classic twentieth century, somewhat worn and battered. She had hardly spoken to Jack in the general stir of arrival, and now looked over toward him, standing with a jug of martinis in his hand, much less nervous here in his own lair than he had been at Hallie Summerson's. The tic had vanished for the moment. Could Carryl Cope have put him off on that occasion? For Jack was obviously rooted in a background, New England, money, Lucy guessed, at any rate taste, the assurance of a born gentleman and scholar. Whereas Carryl Cope seemed suspended in an element of her own creation and it had nothing whatever to do with her background, in fact she appeared to have none that one could place. She spoke academese, a language that springs like Athene from an intellectual brow, and she spoke it with a non-regional, "good" accent.

"How's Olive these days?" Jack asked the President when there was a convenient pause.

"Well, she's getting old, you know. It seems impossible to believe, but she really is." There was a twinkle in Tillotson's eye.

"How does it show?"

"She's irritable, touchy, and has taken to changing her will at the drop of a hat."

"Or at the hiring of a psychiatrist?" Jack and Tillotson chuckled. The President turned politely to Lucy and the Atwoods.

"Perhaps you haven't yet heard of Olive Hunt, but you will."

"You will," Jack repeated gaily, "you will!"

"Impossible old snob!" Maria spoke with characteristic violence.

"Oh Maria, that's not quite fair," Jack answered at once. "She's . . ." He broke off in midair, set his jug down on the mantelpiece, and rocked slightly on his heels. "She's not as easy to describe as I thought. What would you say, Blake?"

Blake Tillotson leaned back in his chair. "Every college has one, I suppose. She's the off-campus power. She lives in the town, a member of the board of trustees."

"And she's Carryl's friend, don't forget that," Maria added. What exactly did that mean, Lucy wondered.

"Give Carryl credit," Jack said quickly, "she never would go and live with Olive. Said she couldn't afford to be rich." He smiled fleetingly at Lucy. "*That*, by the way is one of the college *mots*. You'll hear it again."

"Why couldn't she afford to be rich?"

"She said it cut you off from life—and added, if I was accurately informed, 'look at Olive!'"

"What a person!" Debby was sitting on the floor again. And Lucy, through her haze of martinis and enjoyment, made up a rhyme silently, "People who sit on the floor are a bore."

"Well," Blake Tillotson put his fingers together in a judicial Gothic arch, "like all characters as pronounced as hers, she has the defects of her qualities. She is violently opposed to our hiring a resident psychiatrist, but she wouldn't go so far as to change her will. I trust not. At present she is content with badgering me on the telephone."

"It's disgraceful that she should take your time," Maria said.

"You see, it is a question of belief. One has to respect that." (Nice man, Lucy thought, a thoroughly nice man.)

"Why is Miss Hunt so against a psychiatrist?" Lucy was interested.

"She comes of the old-fashioned school which thinks you pull yourself up by your own bootstraps."

Jack chortled, and then explained himself. "I was just thinking of those actual boots of Olive's, do you remember? Girl-of-the-Limberlost stuff, a plaid jacket, khaki riding pants, and high laced boots. Good Lord, I'd forgotten all about them. And the old felt hat, her father's no doubt." Jack's face was pink with laughter.

But Blake Tillotson went on quietly with his train of thought. "I suspect that she may have had some sort of breakdown herself, after her father's death, and that she pulled herself out of it on sheer guts."

"And on Carryl Cope's guts!" Jack interrupted. "She used to call Carryl up in the middle of the night, demand her presence, got Carryl to teach her Latin."

"She does sound like rather a problem," Henry Atwood said, his eyes bright with interest.

"She's definite," Blake Tillotson mused, "and that can be a problem, but she's also generous; she's violent, but she suffers for it afterwards, and actually apologizes for the scenes she makes; and, above all, we must admit," he turned more aggressively and specifically toward Maria, "she cares deeply about Appleton."

"Time for food," Jack said, seeing that his wife was suspended at the door of the dining room, waiting for a pause, "But let me just say before all this gets written indelibly into the Atwoods' and Miss Winter's record: she's a brilliant woman, and a very kind one."

"Hear, hear!" Maria shouted too loudly. "Come and get your plates, please. The fact is," she murmured to Lucy, who had been the first to rise, "that she adores Jack, and he is flattered."

"She does not adore me," and for the first time he sounded irritated, "but it's a relief to talk to someone who is really interested in what I'm doing."

Lucy, digging into a huge bowl of paella, spooning out clams, rice, pieces of lobster, was aware of the live current that had just sparked between these two. At moments such as this she missed John frightfully, felt as if she were cut in two and were dangling dangerously in thin air. It came on like toothache, the sharp pain, under her careful listening to Jack as he told her that he had been translating some of Valéry's poems and had found in Olive Hunt an acute critic. She helped herself to French bread, and salad, and then went and sat down beside Blake Tillotson, forcing her attention to the moment and away from the dangerous martini-induced operation of memory.

"You said just now that every college has an Olive Hunt, and the other day Hallie Summerson explained that every college has a pet radical. What are some of the other species, Dr. Tillotson?"

"A rather dangerous question, Miss Winter," and he

smiled his shrewd smile of an old turtle, not to be drawn out.

"The professional rebel, usually a student, usually a bright one," Jack took her up.

"The good gray professor who has to be carried long past her—or his—time," Maria added.

Blake Tillotson, who had winced slightly at this one, said quickly, "And surely the old janitor or groundsman who has total recall."

The laughter of recognition was followed by a silence, the silence that good food brings in its wake.

"What a wonderful feast, Maria!" Debby led a chorus of approval, and for once the imperturbable Maria looked shy.

"Well," she explained, "it came out all right. You know why?" She shrugged her shoulders. "The boys have gone to their granny for the weekend. I could concentrate. You know, Jack," she turned to her husband with an intimate smile, "it's amazing the difference it makes. No Giorgio to make me feel anxious about the rice because he stirs it so much and feels so anxious himself; no Pietro to beg me not to murder the lobsters, and to scream when I put them into the water, no Stephen for me to stumble over!"

"They sound wonderful!" It occurred to Lucy that she would never never settle for being a female oddity, a professor, and give up all this, this nervous thread that pulled taut between Jack and Maria, the bicycle in the hall, the little boys, the rich expansive complex web of a family.

Then, before she was aware of how it began, they were off on a discussion of religion. At first she was amused. Hadn't she read somewhere that after a good meal the talk invariably turned to God? Then she looked around her and noticed the tension on all the faces, the absent look, the look of something like discomfort or fear as if, as they sat here in the small room, the roof had just blown off and an uncomforting huge sky opened over their heads. She had been aware of the studied avoidance of intensity at Appleton. Even Hallie had chosen to speak ironically of her political beliefs. Now with the mention of Traherne, and then of Simone Weil—those opposite poles—they all grew tense. Debby said with her unfailing brightness:

"She was rather a neurotic, wasn't she? All those headaches . . ."

"You ask the saint to be normal?" Maria asked, turning the full vehemence of her personality toward Debby with the utmost scorn. Lucy was fascinated to sense real commitment here, perhaps for the first time. "Don't you see, she was maintaining an almost impossible suspension between two worlds, determined to stand at the intersection of faith and non-faith, or rather the Church and the believers outside it, what could be more painful?" Maria shrugged. "Oh, an unpleasant person, of course, no charm," she said angrily. "She was in extremity. Does it cost nothing to be a saint?"

Henry looked embarrassed, but whether on his wife's account or on Maria's one did not know. He said earnestly, "But Traherne was not in extremity. He was purely joyous.

It seems to me that the joy has gone out of religion, and without joy, what is it?"

Lucy saw the fine edge under the banker's mask, the tension just under the skin as Tillotson answered, "An endless struggle to believe without giving up the intellect, an endless struggle to relate mystery and reason. What was easy for Traherne, because he did not need to face it, has become hard for us."

"But why do we feel this need to believe?" Jack asked. He had gone out for a moment and come back with a French book in his hand. "After all, we're not children. Why this sense of absence? I find it embarrassing." Lucy noticed that the nervous tic had come back.

"What seems to me embarrassing is to watch a generation coming into college who have gone back to Traherne's simple faith. This, if you will forgive me, Henry, does seem like a regression." Tillotson leaned forward and, though he smiled, he was clearly in earnest. "My own instinct, I am afraid, is to inject doubt."

"Very dangerous, Blake," Maria teased gently.

"Believe me, I lie awake at night over this." And he turned back to Henry, who had his characteristic expression of innocent amazement. "We have daily chapel, you may have noticed. That is by student request, and they run it themselves. I sometimes imagine the ghost of Miss Wellington hovering about in a state of extreme displeasure . . ." he ended with a laugh.

"I find Péguy useful," Jack said. "He's full of unacceptable simple truths. You can't fail to understand what he is talking about, nor fail to find it disturbing."

"Of course what we teach them," Blake Tillotson went on, "and not only in the social sciences, is that all values are relative. They feel that they have no underpinning; they are scared to death."

"And so they run home to God?" Lucy heard herself say, "Or rather to a God who died in the late nineteenth century, the one with a long white beard?" She was dismayed to recognize it as an echo of John's voice, of John's attitude, and she was struck by how much she had changed in five years. What did she believe in now?

"And when there ain't no home to run to, they have nervous breakdowns and we call in a professional psychiatrist to hold their psyches together." Blake Tillotson shrugged his shoulders. It was a defeatist gesture, a strange gesture for this heavy-set man to make, and one which seemed out of character.

"Let me read you what I went into the study to find," Jack said, still standing in the doorway. "It's a passage from Simone Weil. I'll make a rough translation as I go along: 'Two prisoners in contingent cells, who communicate by blows struck on the wall. The wall is what separates them, but also what permits them to communicate. So it is with us and God. Every separation is a bond.'"

Lucy felt that each of them, including herself, went off with this powerful image like a dog with a bone to bury it in his own private garden for future use; at any rate the audible discussion came to an end. And it was a relief when Maria suggested that they listen to some Bach. While the familiar Prelude and Fugue in C Minor climbed all around them, as if a cathedral were being built in the air, Lucy thought, she found herself considering the last sentence, "Every separation is a bond." What did it mean? Or was it one of those gnomic phrases which penetrate to a layer of consciousness below reason, that one recognizes without being able to define? The wall that had separated John and herself was, she saw, in the clarity made possible by Bach's relentless musical precision, the scientific approach versus the intuitive one, the old old war which might in the last analysis be the war between men and women. By what language then might she and John have knocked their message of love through it? Sex had not been the answer, after all. Where there is no true mutuality, sex ends by being only another expression of hostility. We failed, Lucy thought, miserably. We failed each other.

"A penny for your thoughts, Lucy." Maria startled Lucy out of her revery. What could she answer?

"I was thinking that all this puts an immense weight on human love," she said.

CHAPTER 5

A few days later the faculty was called to a special meeting, and Lucy made her way into the Victorian amphitheatre, curious to witness this gathering of the clan and to have her initiation into Appleton at its most formal and formidable. The semicircular room did have a certain charm with its carved oak decorations and stiff-backed wooden benches. The President and two Deans were seated on Gothic thrones between life-size plaster casts of Pallas Athene and Apollo. Lucy had met the academic Dean only once, a handsome middle-aged woman with a rather hard surface, enhanced by jet-black hair, Miss Valentine by name. The Dean of the College, an elderly pencil-thin lady (very definitely "a lady") was rumored to have a sense of humor; at the moment she looked merely patient. Turning from the stage to the auditorium—where the faculty was still sauntering in like an audience at a play—Lucy was surprised to see how many men there were, after all, on the roster of this college which remained indomitably feminine and feminist. Blake Tillotson now made his way to the lectern and stood, waiting affably, for the menagerie to settle down.

"When Miss Cope is ready to give me the floor—" he chaffed. Caryl Cope was standing in the aisle surrounded by an animated group.

"I *beg* your pardon, Blake," she said airily, and sat down, while the ripple of laughter subsided.

"For the benefit of those of you who are new among us, let me remind you that no student is expelled from Appleton without a majority vote by the faculty, and that the faculty is not called into special session on such a matter without a recommendation from student government. I realize how busy you all are, so we shall hope to make this brief. Miss Valentine, will you present the case?"

Miss Valentine, replacing the President at the lectern, was visibly tense. She had a rather flat voice and this, or possibly the attitude it revealed, which was one of controlled irritation, Lucy found chilling. The case concerned Agnes Skeffington, a Senior who had been, it appeared, a model student, able in all her work, brilliant in the field of mathematics. But lately she had become absorbed in a mathematical problem, to the exclusion of every other responsibility. She had cut most of her classes, even in

Carryl Cope's advanced mediaeval history (this, Lucy suspected, might be *lèse-majesté*); she had handed in no papers; had failed to appear at any of the meetings of a House Committee of which she was presiding officer; "in fact," Miss Valentine ended, "she has, to all intents and purposes, withdrawn from the college. I have had several talks with her, and her attitude remains adamant; she will make up required work *when* she has completed the problem which, she insists, demands her undivided attention at present."

Miss Valentine sat down and stared grimly out at the faculty, while Blake Tillotson opened the meeting to comment and discussion. He recognized first an elderly professor, dressed in rough blue tweed, with a shock of white hair that stood up like a cock's comb, Professor March of the Department of Mathematics. His charm, that of the darling male professor at a woman's college, was evident at once. He commended Miss Valentine at some length "on the very clear picture she has given us of this interesting case." He went on, elaborately, by reminding them of the old story of the Christian thrown to the lions, whom the lions refused to devour as he whispered a message into their ears. The something was, as he was sure they remembered, "After the meal, you will have to make an after-dinner speech, you know." Mild laughter suggested that they did indeed remember. When it had subsided, Professor March went on, "I feel that I am facing a rather formidable row of lions here. Agnes, as you all know, is my student. May I just whisper in your ears this little message: If we let her go, I have no doubt that Radcliffe will welcome her to the fold."

When the delighted laughter had subsided, and Professor March had sat down again, Miss Valentine asked, "What makes you think, Professor March, that Radcliffe would welcome a student who is failing all her courses except one?"

"My dear Miss Valentine," the Professor stood and beamed, "I am aware that this is a very unorthodox student, one who must be trying to the administration, to say the least, as also to her other professors" (here a faint bow in Carryl Cope's direction was discernible), "but let me say simply that mathematical genius is also unorthodox."

"Would you say that Agnes had mathematical *genius*? Would you go as far as that, Professor?" The President, Lucy sensed, was on the student's side.

"She has only been able to concentrate for the last few weeks, since her demission from the college, as you are all aware . . ." He waited for the murmur of laughter. "I would go so far as to say that this girl is capable of original work."

"And that is unusual?" Tillotson pressed.

Professor March shrugged. "Among female students so rare I can say it has never happened before in my twenty years here. In ten years at Columbia, I had two male students of whom I could say as much."

He sat down.

Lucy looked anxiously in Carryl Cope's direction. Surely

she would not remain silent? But Blake Tillotson recognized first a young woman in the Department of Physics. She felt strongly that in a liberal arts college, students should be required to complete work in several fields. If the girl was that brilliant, she could go on to graduate school and concentrate there; open rebellion was not to be tolerated. She was followed by a young man with a foreign accent who pleaded the danger of favoritism. If they began to make exceptions, where would it end? He himself had a student who was engaged in writing a novel, but he had not seen his way to excusing her from a term paper on that account. By this time Lucy had wavered back and forth and did not know what she thought. She felt that the sense of the meeting had shifted and that the majority at present would stand, though reluctantly, against Agnes Skeffington. So it was at a moment of considerable tension that Carryl Cope at last took the floor.

"As you all know," she began, every word meticulously articulated in her deep voice, "Agnes Skeffington is—or was, until she disappeared into a cloud of figures—a student of mine. Let me make it crystal clear that I do not give a hoot whether she comes to my class or not, if she is doing distinguished work in another field." The two young professors seated just in front of Lucy exchanged an eager wink and nod. This is what they had learned to expect of Carryl Cope, evidently, and Lucy felt ashamed of her own circumspection. "The point is, my friends," and now she turned toward her colleagues rather than toward the stage, "that we talk a great deal about excellence, and pride ourselves on demanding it, but when we get what we have asked for, become as confused and jejeune as a freshman in a course on ethics. We are unwilling, evidently, to pay the price of excellence. What is the price?" and here she turned to the stage and addressed her final remarks to Miss Valentine (so Lucy sensed). "The price is eccentricity, maladjustment if you will, isolation of one sort or another, strangeness, narrowness. Excellence costs a great deal. It is high time some of us faced the fact."

Lucy would have liked to shout "Bravo!" No one went so far, but there was an impish stir, a chuckled wave of response, even a few scattered clappings of hands, as Carryl Cope sat down. The President had not been able to conceal a smile, nor Miss Valentine a frown.

"Would anyone like to add a word to the discussion, or is your pleasure that we put the matter to a vote? Would someone like to make a motion?"

Lucy was not surprised to see Miss Finch slowly rise to her feet from far back in the room. As usual she took her time.

"If we should make an exception to our perfectly good rules and standards in this special case, may I suggest that we write into the body of our law a new rule that would cover such cases in the future? My thought is . . ." Miss Finch paused here while she formulated her thought, "that we might incorporate an amendment: In the case of work above and beyond the usual college standard, a student shall be allowed a specific period of freedom from her usual obligations, *provided*," and here Miss Finch's voice became decisive, "she has fulfilled those obligations by the time she graduates. I agree with Mr. Simonides that graduation from Appleton must imply a general education, a general culture. It would present a real hazard if we were to add one to the growing number of pure scientists who have no humanistic foundation."

How serious it all is, Lucy thought, and her feelings were compounded of something like awe before the power they must assume toward a human destiny, and a disgraceful impulse to laugh. As soon as one was not personally involved, how easy to be detached! But into the corner of her thought there crept also the image of Agnes Skeffington herself . . . stubborn, brilliant, knowing what she wanted, able to defy even Carryl Cope by sheer belief. What extremity of being must exist in a young woman with such faith in herself! Lucy's contemplation of it filled her with humility. She herself had never in her life been seized by anything as wholeheartedly as that. And shall I ever be, she wondered? Am I capable of such commitment?

The vote itself was close, even with Miss Finch's proviso incorporated into the motion. But in the final count, the ayes had a majority. Agnes Skeffington would be allowed to go her lonely way within the college.

Miss Valentine was visibly annoyed; she walked off the stage and disappeared. The President and the Dean of the college came down through the auditorium, on the other hand, stopping to talk. Lucy found herself squeezed into the crowd, directly in front of Carryl Cope, and was very much surprised to be tapped on the shoulder by that august hand, and invited to "come back with me and have a drink? It's a suitable hour, is it not?"

As they drove along in Miss Cope's Hillman she explained that the old house where she had an apartment had belonged originally to the owners of a textile factory, rivals of Eben Wellington whose daughter had founded the college. And indeed it was imposing, set back in a large garden that resembled a park, a late Victorian house with long narrow windows, a mansard roof, painted battleship gray. "The remaining Woodwards, two maiden ladies, live downstairs. We treat them like Venetian glass, as Blake hopes to get the house for the college, eventually . . ."

The private entrance, hidden at one side, and the narrow stairway up two flights, had not prepared Lucy for the spaciousness that opened out as they arrived. She stepped into a long high room that might have been an eighteenth-century gentleman's library. What a contrast to Hallie's unselfconscious accumulation of family furniture, plants and books! This room had evidently been designed as the reflection of a highly selfconscious personality. Red damask curtains swept to the floor at three windows, the walls between them lined from top to bottom with books, many of them in fine bindings, and in many languages. The room was dominated by a huge refectory table with heavy carved legs, littered with papers, paperback detective stories, a French novel, as well as some formidable leather-bound tomes. An elaborate marble mantel at the far end of the room drew Lucy's attention to the painting that hung above it, a study of clouds blowing across a blue sky, the clouds of a damp country, reforming themselves, all in motion—England, Lucy supposed. She made her way across the room to take a closer look, just as Carryl Cope came back with a tray containing a bowl of olives and two martinis.

"Ah, you are looking at the Constable. Charming, isn't it? It belongs to Olive Hunt, actually; she saw I had fallen in love with it, and kindly lent it to me. By the way, Olive may drop in later on. She often does. Says she likes my martinis. Have one."

The atmosphere was cordial, so much so that Lucy wondered whether there were not some special reason for such attention to a temporary instructor in a different department. She felt absurdly nervous, and was dismayed to find her hand shaking as she took the martini glass.

"The spectacle you have just witnessed must have been entertaining for you?" But just as Lucy was registering how pompous Carryl Cope did sound, the tone changed. "Good gracious, child, don't sit in that uncomfortable chair! Come here where I can see you!"

She sat down obediently in a red leather armchair directly opposite the small imperious figure on the sofa. "Well?"

"Well what?"

"Were you entertained?"

"In a way," Lucy said warily. "I'm so new at all this. I

suppose I'm torn between awe and laughter." She caught the slight wince. "I thought you were splendid."

"Damn fool! I should have kept my trap shut. Jennifer saved the day with that exquisite judicial mind of hers." Then, having given the devil his due, she added, "I can't say I like Agnes Skeffington, though. Genius is always intolerable when you come right down to it. Don't you agree?"

"I haven't had much experience with genius."

"Not that young doctor?" But, catching Lucy's look of dismay, Carryl Cope quickly added, "Very rude of me, to mention your private affairs. But you might as well get used to living in a goldfish bowl."

"I was only startled," Lucy said at once. "I try not to think about John." Then she suddenly laughed. "But he's not a genius, anyway, though he is maddening, of course."

"In what way, if I may be permitted to press on?"

Lucy felt a great longing to talk about John, and a fear of doing it, a fear of exposing herself to this woman's curiosity and, worse, to her perspicacity which Lucy suspected might be something like John's—irrefutably there, but also at times besides the point. And his entrance into the room, the return of his presence at just this moment, was painful. One does not bury the past, she thought; one lives with it. "I'm sorry," she said, feeling the pause becoming embarrassingly long. "I find it hard to formulate. Maybe one of our points of contention was that he is interested in the general, the abstract, and I in the specific and the personal. His language itself used to madden me," and she smiled.

Carryl Cope laughed. "I never can understand why women expect men to be like themselves."

"Anyway, it's all over. We do not even write." Liquor is quicker, she thought, dismayed by the acute pain she felt in the middle of her chest. "I think we really loved each other, but somehow we could never communicate, so it ended by becoming like an illness."

"And you are convalescing here?" The challenge in the faintly mocking air was beginning to be familiar. "You are not really committed to us, are you?"

"I don't know," Lucy said, balking at being pinned down. "I don't think I'm a very good teacher, at present. But perhaps I should not have been a very good wife." She said this lightly, but it boomeranged and hurt as it reverberated in her heart.

"You are a rather curious phenomenon. It's unusual to go through the labor of getting a Doctor's degree unless one is serious. Were you? Or did you want to marry that John of yours? Was that the main thing?"

"That was the main thing," Lucy said, forced to honesty though she knew she was being disappointing. "Isn't that serious enough for you?"

Carryl Cope got up and took the tray of glasses out to the kitchen. She had not responded to this little prick, and Lucy wondered if she were offended, but she herself was on her mettle now.

"You have never regretted not marrying?" she asked,

standing in the door of the kitchen. It was odd that they both took it for granted that marriage and the sort of prestige Carryl Cope represented were generally found to be incompatible.

"No." The answer was definite. "When I was young no one wanted to marry me; and when I was old, I wanted to marry no one. Here you are, Dr. Winter." Lucy was handed a second martini and this time the "Dr." was heavily ironic.

"I must seem to you slightly ridiculous."

"My dear child," the tone was irritable, "it is I who am ridiculous. In my heart of hearts I have to agree that the intellectual woman, as Dr. Johnson said of the woman preacher, can only be compared to a dog standing on its hind legs."

"Yet you have given your life to persuading generations of students of just the opposite . . ."

"No, I teach for the singular, for the exceptional; I teach for the one in a hundred, one in a thousand maybe. And you forget," the tiger glared, "that teaching is only half my life; my work is still, don't you know, quite extraordinarily absorbing. I sometimes think I am just beginning to discover what it is all about . . ." This last was said so modestly that Lucy was touched. "Good God! Without my own work I would go mad. It gives me some nourishment at the roots." Then she smiled and recovered herself; the eyes that had flashed out became hooded and withdrawn. "I get awfully angry with my work, want to throw it out the window and read a detective story. What people will not understand about our profession as teachers," she said, walking up and down the length of the room, "is that it takes the marrow out of your bones, and something or other has to put it back. For me, work does that. Where is Olive?" she asked suddenly, and Lucy suspected that it was not a *non sequitur*, but that Carryl Cope also required nourishment of a more personal kind. "I suppose you have an idea that all is peace and quiet, that this is a safe little grove without a faun or a fury in it, just a collection of (we hope!) brilliant old maids, a sort of secular retreat where perpetually active minds perpetually sow seeds in virgin ground."

Lucy smiled. "Well," she said cautiously, "I wouldn't say quite that, though the ground is virgin all right—and it does seem rather safe."

"Safe?"

Carryl Cope walked over to the window. She looked very small, standing against the long crimson curtains, small and tired. "Safe?" she asked again and turned back, thrusting her hands into her pockets. "My dear child, if you could, for one moment, look into the lives around you . . ."

"How I would like to!"

"Did it ever cross your innocent mind that people with no personal lives, no passions, no conflicts could not possibly do the sort of teaching an institution of this kind demands? What do you think we are?"

A momentary vision crossed Lucy's mind of flocks of professors dashing off to Italy or Greece on sabbatical leave, to have love affairs with D. H. Lawrence game-keepers or fishermen, and she could not swallow the delighted smile the vision evoked.

"Oh well, smile." Carryl Cope shrugged it off, as if Lucy were beyond the pale.

At this moment of possible revelation, or confidence, she was sorry to hear the muted ring of the doorbell; Carryl murmured, "Excuse me. That will be Olive. Where *have* you been?" Lucy registered the cross, intimate inflection as she rose to her feet to confront Olive Hunt (whom every college has, she remembered, but surely not always just like this!) She shook hands with a rangy, gray-haired woman with piercing blue eyes, an emaciated face that must once have been beautiful, in a tweed suit with a diamond sunburst at her throat, long elegant feet and hands.

"Olive, this is our new instructor, Dr. Winter, of the English department."

"Harriet has told me about you," she said brusquely; she was evidently full of some preoccupation of her own, and hardly looked at Lucy. "I've been having another wrangle with Blake," she announced to the room at large, for Carryl had disappeared down the hall. "It is a mystery to me why perfectly good people who have no reason to let themselves be bamboozled, end by listening to fools and charlatans."

"Blake listens to you, dear." Carryl stood in the door, shining with mockery and pleasure. "Drink this and calm down."

"I won't calm down!" But she laughed, then sat down abruptly, stretched out her long slim legs, crossed at the ankles, and fixed her piercing blue gaze on Lucy. "Forgive me. I am, as you can see, exercised."

"All colleges have them," Carryl murmured, "after all." Lucy presumed that the personal pronoun must refer, not to elderly ladies on the Board of Trustees, but to resident psychiatrists. The subject kept coming up, she noticed.

"Appleton has never conformed, Carryl, as you very well know. We had three communists on the faculty during that McCarthy business," she explained to Lucy, with a toss of her head, "and a damn nuisance they were, I must say."

"Harriet is certainly not, and never was, a communist," Carryl said sharply.

"Oh well," Olive shrugged this off, "she might as well have been for all the trouble we had about her."

For an instant Carryl Cope looked as if she were going to be angry, then gave Olive a queer little glance, half commiserating, half irritated. "You know, when you come right down to it, Olive, this is none of your business." Lucy sensed that their relationship thrived on this sort of banter, and especially when the banter had an edge. "The trustees do not make faculty appointments."

"None would be made over our unanimous veto."

"You couldn't possibly get it," Carryl needled. "I don't think you realize quite how old-fashioned you and I have become."

"My dear child, what the girls need is not more 'help'—

ugh, how I loathe that word!—but greater demands on their intellects and souls. I expect that last word has no meaning to one of your generation, Dr. Winter?"

"I'd probably use the word 'psyche,' but not for any good reason. I must admit, though, that a resident psychiatrist seems to me not a bad idea."

"Why?"

Lucy was not going to let herself be daunted by a diamond sunburst and the ineffable air of authority that rises like a cloud from those who possess large trust funds. "For one thing because I don't believe in professors having to take on the students' personal problems."

"Hear, hear!" Carryl Cope uttered loudly.

"No one expects you to."

"No, maybe not. But it happens that you find yourself face to face with a problem, willy nilly. I have a Freshman whom I dread to see in conference because she is clearly incapacitated by some private woe."

"How do you know? Perhaps she is just lazy, or going through a phase."

"I know because the girl appears in class in a state of alarming self-neglect, dirty, hair hardly brushed; because she keeps her head down throughout the hour, and because it is clear that she spends a great deal of time crying."

"So did I when I was her age," Olive said, unexpectedly. "I suspect that I rather enjoyed it. I got out of it, not because I had a professor who took a personal interest in me, but because I did have (thank God!) a professor who made me take an interest in a subject. It happened to be Greek. Give her psychiatric attention—for I presume what you are saying is that you would be glad to turn this weeper over to someone else and take her back when she combs her hair and stops crying—give her *that*, and she'll just wallow in *self*."

Lucy cast a questioning glance in Carryl Cope's direction, but it gave her no clue.

"Maybe I'm just not a very good teacher," Lucy said with her back to the wall. "But she is not at the moment capable of reading *The Iliad*, let alone getting interested in it."

"The translations are inadequate." Lucy felt baffled by this assault from temperament, originality, and non-reason in equal quantities.

" 'The best lack all conviction, while the worst are full of passionate intensity,' " Carryl Cope quoted the much-quoted, but Lucy was happy to hear Yeats invoked in this room, which he would have enjoyed, as well as the personality it reflected, learned, curious, wearing a mask of mockery to conceal—what? Lucy liked Carryl Cope; she did not dislike Olive Hunt, but she found her truly eccentric, off-center. She had, Lucy suspected, led a wholly undisciplined and self-indulgent life, though nothing would astonish her more than to be told so. Probably she got up at six and either did physical exercises or spiritual ones, mortified herself in idiosyncratic ways, and thought because of this that she had a disciplined mind and knew what a life like Carryl Cope's, so much more demanding in every way, was all about.

Had Carryl's point of view been colored by *this* influence? Was this her vulnerability, her Achilles heel, an attachment that provided a Constable over the mantel and these passionate tensions, and what else? How dangerous love can be, Lucy thought, while the discussion continued between the other two. She came back to it to hear Miss Hunt saying, in an apparent total reversal from her position earlier on.

"Is the subject the point? Isn't it a means to an end? And isn't the end of teaching to bring people up, to get that sordid Freshman of yours onto her feet and functioning as a human being? So it's no excuse," she turned back to Lucy with a fleeting smile, "to say she can't read *The Iliad.* It's all woven together, surely. But you want to split people up, hand over part of your student to a psychiatrist while you stuff her noodle with information. I call that abdicating!"

"Olive, you are being rather hard on Lucy." Carryl Cope used her given name for the first time and Lucy was pleased. "Of course, there are students who simply do not belong in college. This girl sounds like one of those. Oh dear, do let's change the subject. I feel quite winded!"

"But let me just answer!"

"Don't shoot till you see the whites of her eyes!" Carryl laughed.

But Lucy felt too badgered and on the defensive to take things lightly. "I think you're probably right," she said turning to Olive Hunt. "Of course one tries to reach the whole person, but if I began to see my students outside the conferences, I wouldn't have time to read their papers or to prepare my classes. Besides," plunging recklessly into the center of the problem again, "don't you think it's dangerous to get personally involved?"

The blue eyes narrowed. "Dangerous? Pish-tush!"

"How are they going to learn anything about feeling if they don't feel?" Carryl Cope was suddenly really involved, Lucy felt, almost angry. "The trouble with all of you is that you have acquired a set of formulas that make it possible for you to reduce life to a mechanism. We are all a little in love with our teachers, and a very good thing too."

Lucy felt an immense gulf between herself and these two powerful and powerfully unconscious women, the gulf of the generation, and she decided it was time to go. She got up, glancing at her watch. "I really must tear myself away," she said awkwardly, not knowing quite how to leave. "Those freshman papers . . ."

"Oh dear, must you? Just when things began to get tense," Carryl Cope teased. "But you have to sit down for five minutes. I want to speak of Jane Seaman before you go."

So—that was it, the real reason behind the invitation. Carryl Cope had showed her hand at last.

"What about Jane?" Lucy said, still nettled and prickly, "she appears to be everything one could possibly hope for in a student. And *she* makes no personal demands."

"We've rubbed Lucy the wrong way," Carryl Cope announced with a smile. "Jane is enjoying your course very much, by the way."

"It's a grand class," Lucy responded, glad for a change of subject. "They keep me on my mettle. Jane is doing a paper on Melville's viability as a subject for certain fashionable critical approaches. I must confess this seems to me pretty advanced stuff for her to undertake. The reading it will require is prodigious, but she seemed so very eager to have a try." Then Lucy felt she must say one more thing about what had occurred earlier. "You don't rub me the wrong way. It's just that I feel overwhelmed. I don't see how anyone can be a good teacher, let alone a great one. You can't win: either you care too much or too little; you're too impersonal or too personal; you don't know enough or you bury the students in minutiae; you try to teach them to write an honest sentence, and then discover that what is involved is breaking a psychological block that can only be broken if you take on the role of psychoanalyst, parent, friend—God knows what!" This passionate sally was greeted with laughter. "You laugh, but it's hell!"

"It's all right," Carryl said, still laughing. "We all feel exactly as you do. The relation between student and teacher must be about the most complex and ill-defined there is."

"And that's why you're all so alive here," Lucy said, mollified.

"Or all so dead! But I won't let you go," she added,

as Lucy once more made a move, "without one word more. I do have the idea that Jane is pushing things a bit too hard."

Lucy felt baffled and tired. "Do you think then I should suggest a less difficult subject for her paper?"

"No." Carryl Cope walked over to the windows to draw the curtains. "No," she said thoughtfully, "I just wish you would keep an eye on her."

So even the brilliant student, the paragon, must be watched and tended like a plant, now stimulated by water and sunlight, now placed in the shade temporarily!

"I'll do what I can." Lucy stood in the middle of the room, hesitating between shaking Olive Hunt's hand and waiting for Miss Cope, who was rummaging about at her desk.

"Here, let me just give you this, an advance copy of *Appleton Essays*. Have you seen it before? We are rather proud of this little publication. You might be interested in Jane's analysis of *The Iliad*." The closely printed, solemn-looking pamphlet was placed in Lucy's hands at the door. "I've enjoyed this. Now you have found your way, come again."

"I'd love to."

Lucy ran down the stairs, hearing the deep voice call behind her, "You won't get lost? Take the second turning on the left!"

Lucy took a deep breath as she closed the outside door behind her. It was not dark yet, and there was a smell of leaves and earth, the bitter autumn smell. An avenue of maples stretched before her, and through the clear late sky, a translucent green, she could see one planet shining. She walked slowly, tasting the moment, reluctant to go back to the gloomy faculty house, to the campus gossip around the little tables. She was thinking about the two powerful characters she had just left, and about the in-wardness of their relationship. They had rubbed her the wrong way, she realized, made her feel sparky and tense like a cat whose fur is full of electricity. It was not an unpleasant sensation.

CHAPTER 6

Later that evening Lucy lay on her bed, still dressed, wondering how to summon the energy to get up and turn on her bath. She had found a three-hour stint correcting freshman papers deadening and exhausting. For once there had been no gleam to leaven the lump of dullness and adequacy. She had, apparently, led twenty-five intelligent girls to their first contact with a masterpiece —and simply nothing whatever had taken place to trouble the bland surface of their minds. They managed at best to sound as patronizing toward *The Iliad* as if they had been asked to review a C-grade movie!

Oh, she understood how one might plunge back into one's own work after a session like this, grunting with pleasure at the difficulties it presented like a pig hunting for truffles, how Carryl Cope must go back to that immense desk of hers and prickle with excitement and relief at being alone with her own mind for a change! Whereas all I do, Lucy admonished herself bitterly, is to lie down like lead, or fall into moodiness thinking of John. The name forced her to her feet and she turned her back resolutely on the ghost of John, only to meet him again as soon as she lay in the bath. Naked in the warm water, her sense of deprivation was acute. We are all babies crying for comfort, she reminded herself. Other women have gone this way before me. The contrast between her professional self and this miserable naked rejected woman seemed to her suddenly grotesque. She rubbed herself down hard as if to rub the image away, forced her mind to consider the Freshmen again, "they toil not, neither do they spin," she said aloud, relieved that she could smile, and evoked their round unformed faces, which did after all in a curious way resemble the lilies of the field. I must find some way to reach them, she thought. Rage? A storm? Frighten them into paying attention. She pushed the means aside as unworthy. But the intensity of purpose and belief demanded of her in relation to them staggered her. Who am I to rouse the dead?

She got into bed and picked up the pamphlet Carryl Cope had given her with such obvious pride—well, that ought to put her to sleep! But it proved to be the worst possible choice, for after reading the first page of Jane Seaman's essay, Lucy felt a chill of apprehension run through her, and she read on with increasing dread and

dismay. Was this hallucination? Or had she read almost
the same words, and certainly the same ideas, somewhere
else, just the other day. But where? She had spent an
afternoon reading all sorts of odd essays and books, hoping
to get a new slant on *The Iliad*, to see it freshly for herself before teaching it.

When she laid the pages down, she could not sleep but
lay wideawake in the dark, her mind restlessly leading
her here and there, playing the tricks memory will, the
size of a page or the cover of a book spotlighted suddenly,
then disappearing. Then she thought she was coming
close as the title "The Poem of Force" swam into her
consciousness. But the author escaped her. There was
nothing to be done but wait till she could get to the
library in the morning.

If only it could not be true! Or . . . what if she just
forgot about it? She was not Jane Seaman's conscience.

But she had, as every instructor was asked to do, made
a brief statement of standards and requirements when
she met her classes first. An overt, proved instance of
plagiarism would mean expulsion from the college. For
this there could be no extenuating circumstances. I am
Jane Seaman's instructor, she reminded herself, I do have
a special concern . . . she could see, in her mind's eye,
that lock of fair hair, trained to fall over one eye, could
hear the high clear voice saying, "But Miss Winter,
surely . . ." Lucy had been ashamed of some deep resistance she had always felt about this girl. She had to admit
that, whatever turned out to be the truth about this essay,

Jane had a brilliant mind, and a need to excel so compelling that she would work fiendishly hard to achieve recognition. Why then jeopardize everything she had in her hands by an act that risked so much, like a teller who steals money from a bank? At this moment Jane had become a great deal more interesting and even *simpatica* than she had ever seemed before.

The evidence—a copy of *The Mint*, an English publication which had died in the forties after a few issues—was painfully clear when Lucy finally tracked down in it Simone Weil's essay on "The Iliad, or The Poem of Force." Lucy had discovered it after that dinner at the Beveridges', when Weil's name had come up . . . wouldn't Jack recognize the steal? If only the discovery didn't have to come from me, Lucy thought with a wild hope. She had been sitting, surrounded by students in the library, making a careful paragraph by paragraph comparison of the two essays. She felt as furtive as a criminal; her heart beat so loudly in the hush that she feared it must rouse the bent heads to lift, listen, and accuse. In her slightly hallucinated state of tension, she felt like some messenger of evil in a Greek play, one of those who, if he escapes with his life, is shunned because it was he who brought the news of defeat. How crazy can you get? Lucy asked herself wryly, as she signed for *The Mint* and made her way out into the most serene of November evenings. Quite suddenly the leaves had fallen. One day they were simply gone after a high wind and rain, pasted onto the shiny black macadam of the roads, shuffled together in the gutters. The bare trees floated like seaweed against a pale yellow sky. It smelled like snow, fresh, a new air . . . the winter air. Lucy stood there for a moment on the library steps and breathed it all in.

Then she turned toward Hallie's house, crossing the campus diagonally, past the dingy old biology building, past the chapel, and out onto the street, where she faced the row of white clapboard houses she had come to know so well. A few doors away Jennifer Finch lived with her mother, and around the corner, the Beveridges. The President's house was set back from the road on a slight elevation. In this light it all looked like an engraving of a New England town, perfectly at peace with itself. The white spire of the Unitarian church added the final touch, and once more Lucy found herself wondering how much this seasoned shell contained of thinned-out blood, failure, and despair. Yet at this moment, walking fast, compelled by the burden she carried, she could not deny its beauty, quiet as a balm. Here, surely, turbulent emotion could come to rest, or be decently buried.

Hallie opened the door to her ring. "You're just the person I want to see. Come in and sit by the fire. Chilly out!"

The atmosphere felt so homely and good that the wild doubt crossed Lucy's mind: have I invented the whole thing? She found it hard to speak.

"Sit down," Hallie urged.

"No," Lucy said, standing with her back to the fire. "I can't. I have a problem, Hallie." She held herself fast to the moment, as if when it was gone, she would not be the same; nothing would be the same.

"I thought you looked a bit peaked." Hallie disappeared into the next room and came back with a decanter of sherry and glasses. "Well, what's on your mind?"

"Have you read Jane Seaman's piece in the *Appleton Essays?*"

"I read proof on it. Why?"

"She stole it, almost a complete paraphrase, and in a few places direct quote."

"Are you sure?"

Lucy put the copy of *The Mint*, opened to the crucial page, into Hallie's hands. One glance would be sufficient. But Hallie read on. And Lucy sipped her sherry, feeling the relief of laying her burden, carried through the long night and the long day, upon someone else's shoulders, someone experienced and wise, someone she could trust.

After what seemed an eternity of silence, tempered only by the seethe of a green log on the fire and the loud ticking of a clock, Hallie looked up.

"What I can't understand," she said after gazing off into the distance for a moment, "is what made her do it."

"She's throwing away so much. I keep seeing that face, so closed and sure of itself, and so intelligent, after all."

"Of course, she's a student of yours. I'd forgotten for a moment. My dear, what a horrible thing for you! I *am* sorry!" And her concern was balm. "You didn't need to have this particular problem your first year. Do you know, in my more than twenty years here I can only remember two cases as clearcut as this . . . and neither of them was a Senior, a brilliant student or . . ." and she caught her breath, "one in whom so much has been invested."

"Carryl Cope," Lucy murmured.

"What a mess!"

"What happens now? What does one do?" Then she suddenly remembered. "I wonder if Professor Cope was aware that something might be wrong. She suggested yesterday that I not push Jane too hard, but," Lucy added eagerly, "she's not a student you push. She pushes herself."

"Yes, yes, of course," Hallie said absentmindedly. "Poor Jane!" Then she added, "It is rather inhuman of me, but I must confess that my first thought was for Carryl in all this. You ask about process," she said drily. "The case will have to go to student government, and then to the faculty. At least," Lucy sensed the hesitation, "that is what has always been done."

"If a person is expelled on these grounds," Lucy asked, for she felt now as if she were being pulled out under the first wave of shock by an undertow, pulled out farther than she knew how to handle, "what happens? I mean, could Jane transfer somewhere else? California?"

"I'm afraid not. I think doors would be pretty well closed against her. She is a Senior, after all." Hallie looked old and tired.

The moment of relief at having passed the buck—for that, Lucy saw now, was what she had tried to do—was entirely gone. What if no one had spotted the thing? Wouldn't that have been better? What terrible fate had

Lucy set in motion, thinking only of her own moral dilemma, the discomfort to herself? "I wish I hadn't told you."

"You can't undo something by pretending it never happened. And the more I think about it," Hallie said, lifting her head for the first time, "the more I keep wondering if we are not all responsible. Something has gone wrong somewhere . . ."

They sat in silence for some moments. There seemed nothing to say. Then Lucy got up, needing now to get away, to think, and above all, to go herself and talk to Jane.

"Hallie—" She hesitated, for she laid the problem in Hallie's lap and was now, in effect, about to withdraw it.

"You'd like to talk to Jane," Hallie said after they had exchanged a strained look.

"Don't tell Carryl Cope for another twenty-four hours."

"As you wish," Hallie said. "But you know that you have set a machinery in motion that cannot be stopped now." The tone was firm, even severe.

"Yes," Lucy said. "I know." It was just this knowledge that filled her with dismay. The messenger in the Greek plays was, after all, not responsible, but she was responsible. She had made a choice involving another human being's whole future, had made it, impetuously, out of shock. At the same time Lucy sensed that after their exchanged look Hallie had withdrawn, and that this withdrawal had taken place out of respect. If she had until now been treated rather like a child by a parent, she was now being treated as a colleague. The whole tone of their discourse since Hallie's spontaneous ejaculation of pity and support, "How awful for you," had changed. If Lucy had set the machinery in motion, she must stay at the controls, and the machine had begun to move with vertiginous speed.

A whole scene from the distant past rose up within her and burst, with another of those small explosions she had been suffering from lately, the electric shock of recognition. It was when she was about twelve, and she had seen Edna May, a girl in her class, cheat on an exam, had watched with horrified fascination Edna May pass a note to her best friend, receive an answer, and copy it down. And Lucy had gone to Miss Powers and told the story, feeling sick to her stomach, had told, and had experienced the same temporary relief as when she had laid *The Mint* in Hallie's hands. Then too she had set a machinery in motion, and had felt the machine get out of control. Then too no one had blamed her overtly, even Edna May who wept, repented, and forgot the incident. But she, Lucy, never forgot. She carried around the wound of her own righteousness all that year; she bitterly despised herself. And finally she had broken down and wept—months after everyone else had forgotten the whole thing—had broken down and sobbed out the whole story to her father, had had hysterics in fact, and sat on his lap while he stroked her hair, in a moment of intimacy so rare between them that it seemed once only. He had spoken saving words that once: "Maybe it was a relief to Edna May to be found out. It's true you broke a code, but must you be a slave to codes? It might be more grown-up not to be."

"I must go," she said, wondering how long she had sat there, lost in the past, among those ghosts.

"Yes," Hallie sighed. "Well . . ."

"I'm going to find Jane. Do you know what dorm she is in?"

"Hawthorne, I think. It will be all right," Hallie said, accompanying Lucy to the door, and looking out to the winter sky. "We take things too seriously. The planets still swim overhead. Remember that." She held out her hand then. The firm clasp was meant to transfuse courage, Lucy sensed, but instead communicated panic. Hallie Summerson was more vulnerable than one might have supposed. We all are, Lucy reminded herself. We are all more vulnerable than we can afford to admit.

CHAPTER 7

On second thought Lucy decided to ask Jane to meet her in her office; it was after five and there would be no one dropping in at that time. On the telephone Jane had answered coolly that she was in the middle of a term paper, but would be glad to oblige if Lucy would excuse dungarees. It was hard not to be irritated by the guarded, slightly patronizing tone, as if she, Jane, were condescending to do a blundering professor a favor. And Lucy found the ten minutes' wait in the dismal office excruciating. A single electric-light bulb dangling from the ceiling under a dusty china globe did not help: the room felt more like a cell than ever.

She was standing peering out into the dark, with her back to the door, when she heard sneakered feet running down the hall. Jane had flung a red coat over her blue jeans; she had on a white boy's shirt; she looked disarmingly young.

"I ran," she said, pushing the lock of hair back, "madly curious. What is all this about?" Her composure seemed absolute, and Lucy quailed.

"Sit down," she said quietly. Lucy leaned back in her chair, and for a second, closed her eyes.

"It happens that I teach *The Iliad* this semester; in the course of some desultory reading on the subject, I found that magnificent piece of Simone Weil's in *The Mint*." There was a pause. Lucy stared fixedly out at the naked trees outside and felt tears start. She reacted to this embarrassing emotion at once. "You know the rule. You know what overt plagiarism, in this case a sometimes line-by-line steal, means in any reputable college."

"I'm sorry," the cool voice spoke without a tremor. "I'm afraid I'm in the dark."

Lucy had dreaded tears, anger, recriminations. She had not imagined as a possibility this refusal to admit the facts. She turned to face Jane, who was just in the act of offering her a cigarette; when Lucy refused it, she lit one herself, drew in and exhaled on a long breath.

"All I want to know is why you did it," Lucy said gently. "You are too brilliant to need the support of someone else's ideas. You risked too much. Why?" She was unable to keep the pressure out of her voice, the fatal tremor out.

"I worked rather hard on that essay." The tone was one of noble regret at the cruel ways of the world.

"Listen!" Lucy was sharp. "You are not going to get away with this, Jane. I spent several hours in the library comparing the two essays. You haven't a leg to stand on. Use your head."

"Has it never happened in the course of history that two people have looked at things in the same way?"

"It may have. In this case it did not. You stole Weil's essay . . . and it looked like a safe steal; who would ever happen on that obscure English journal? You didn't know that the essay has been republished, I understand, in a paperback collection recently?" Lucy shot a glance at the impassive face, and felt completely baffled. "I didn't ask you here to argue. I wanted to try to help. If you don't wish to discuss it with me, that is surely your right." Lucy got up to leave. She felt unutterably weary, as if her mouth were filled with ashes. "Damn it, Jane!" she exploded suddenly, "Give yourself a chance!"

There was a considerable pause. Lucy did not look at Jane.

"I never suspected you of sadism."

Lucy felt the flush rise from her throat, the long stain of rage and frustration and shame. It was absurd to be so close to tears. "I can assure you that I deeply regret having ever read that essay. Having done so, it would surely be failing in kindness and in responsibility toward a human being not to speak to you myself."

"All right, I am to beat my breast, confess etc., and then what?" Lucy looked up and met Jane's eyes for the first time. They looked mad rather than human, and they frightened her.

"Sit down, Jane," she commanded. Since there was no response, she herself sat down. "Perhaps I will have a cigarette after all."

A cigarette was produced, lit, and Lucy smoked while the silence grew and grew. Finally she broke it herself. "No one doubts that you have an excellent mind, Jane; no professor could fail to be grateful for the kind of response you make, and for your contributions to a class. I hope you are aware that you have my respect. Otherwise I would not be here. I would simply have turned in the evidence to the powers that be, student government in other words."

"Those self-righteous girl scouts!"

"If that is what they are—and I rather suspect they may be—why did you put yourself in their hands? Why?" Lucy asked again, and she could not keep the exasperation out of her voice any longer.

"You're new here." The tone was acidly patronizing.

"Yes, I'm new. Very well, what is it I can't understand?"

She saw the hands fly up to the forehead and press themselves there, as if to press down some wildness, some violent need to escape. "The pressure." It was said very low, very calmly, but it was repeated three times: "the pressure, the pressure . . ."

"I'm sure it's not easy to achieve what you have achieved

here in four years, nor to sustain it. As Professor Cope would say, one pays a high price for brilliance."

"What does she know?" Lucy felt as if she had flayed the skin off an animal, so quiet the voice, so clear that the person within was screaming. "From the time I first had her as a Sophomore she has been at me to produce, produce, produce. I'm not a machine!"

Lucy heard Carryl Cope's voice, very far away, talking so convincingly about "the price of excellence"—was this it? This voice of hatred, hating everything, most of all itself? Joyless? Driven? Close enough to madness to make one tremble? "The more you do, the more you're expected to do, and each thing has got to be better, always better." The voice went on monotonously, without inflection like an old record turning round and round on the same groove. The eyes that stared out at Lucy now were as hard as stones. The girl stood by the desk with her hands in her pockets, unyielding, with something of the blind courage of a little bull, the blind look in the eye. And Lucy was silent. Now there was nothing to do but listen. "When I came here I was in love with learning, literally. I was like a starving person who finds food. You can't imagine what my parents are like, how crazy anyone seems who wants to read, especially when they're as good a bridge player as I am, especially a girl. When I got here I thought I was in heaven, all that first year; the second year with Professor Cope in mediaeval history was even better. By then I began to feel like a person in my own right. I mean, it mattered to someone how I did, what I thought . . .

Oh well," the sly look came back; the lock of hair fell forward; she shrugged, but for a moment Lucy had seen the girl under the mask, the shaken human being. How do we dare, she thought, touch this? Force it to grow? Perhaps murder it in the process?

"What happened?" Lucy asked very gently. "Please try to tell me."

"Why in hell should I?"

"Because I am here. Because I came to you," Lucy answered, ignoring the insolence of the tone.

"To me *first?*"

The question was a sneer; it crept through Lucy like a poison. But it had to be answered. The risk was very great, but it had to be answered with the truth.

"No, I talked first to Professor Summerson."

"So," Jane said with a sort of triumph. "It's all over campus by now." She sat down, hugging her knees, rocking slightly, her chin bumping them with the same compulsive rhythm her words had expressed earlier.

"I'm quite sure not."

"You don't know this place."

"I trust Hallie Summerson."

"Oh, she's a good enough egg, but she'll have to tell Carryl Cope. You know that as well as I do."

Somehow in the last few minutes, Lucy had lost the initiative. "Jane," she said with an effort, "we both know that it's not in my power to stop what has been set in motion."

"Why did you come then? What is all this about?"

"Let me try to tell you." Lucy paused, and said something like a prayer for a wisdom she did not possess, for some act of grace she could not imagine. "Maybe I felt that now for a little while we could stand in a small human space as two human beings, and that if I could understand what was back of an act of pure folly (for surely it was that) I might be able to help when—in a day or so—the world steps in, the law, the code, the machinery if you will, takes over."

"Give me a sedative before throwing me to the wolves?"

For the first time Lucy felt anger rising in her. "Has it occurred to you, Jane, that you are throwing Carryl Cope to the wolves? She gave me that issue of *Appleton Essays* with particular pride."

"What a sell for her! The infant prodigy turns out to be a fake!"

"No!" Lucy saw Jane wince and straighten up before the severity of the tone. "There is absolutely no doubt in my mind about your quality as a student. You are not a fake."

"A thief then."

"If you will," for on this point Lucy would not yield. "Why did you do it?"

"Nausea." The sneer was still there.

"I don't understand."

"I just got tired of being pushed so hard, tired of the whole racket, tired of having a brain, tired of coming up to the jump and taking it again and again. Lost my nerve."

The words came out hard and flat. Where did one go from here?

"You've been doing extremely good work, distinguished work for me, Jane."

"Yes, I can always make it at first. Then people begin to ask for more and more. Then I can't make it. Just like a jump, don't you see? The bars go higher and higher. It's crazy." The voice was the shrill voice of a child, and broke. And Lucy remembered, in the sheer relief of the break, the moment when the rain comes in California, when the long winter drought breaks and the hills green over. For the first time since she had confronted Jane, it was possible to get up, go over, and lay a firm hand on her shoulder.

But, at the touch, the fierce little animal and its pride rose up again. "Now you've got what you wanted, leave me alone!" What Lucy heard was not the words but the cry for help underneath them. She walked over to the window and looked out, and waited for the sobs to space themselves and slowly quiet down. "Is there someone you could talk to, Jane? I know I'm not much use . . ."

"At least, you're not fossilized like the others!"

"You've got to go through this now, and it's going to be tough. But you will not be alone, Jane. People care, you know." Lucy was surprised to discover that she herself cared more than she would have thought possible a half hour ago. "It must be a relief to have this out in the open." Then Lucy hesitated, wondering whether she had the right to hazard a guess. But she decided to take the risk. "Perhaps you wanted, without knowing that was what you wanted, to *be* found out, because then the spiral could be broken."

"Maybe," said a small humble voice. "Yes, that's true, I guess." Jane blew her nose loudly and gave a wan smile.

Lucy felt she had been in this room for hours, for weeks, that she had been wrestling with powers and demons far beyond her wisdom to know how to handle, or even to understand. How small, crumpled, and how very young Jane looked, bent over on the chair, hugging herself. "Don't hesitate to come to the Faculty Club any time. I'll always be there if you need me."

Then, without waiting for an answer, Lucy left the office and closed the door behind her. Let Jane take her time. At least, there, she would be alone.

The relief of getting away! The relief of stepping out into the ordinary air of evening, of passing groups of girls laughing and calling out to each other, as if nothing had happened. For the impact of the last hour, and the impact on herself of this role of inquisitor and judge had been greater than she knew at the time; she found that her knees were trembling.

It had been made abundantly clear in the last hour that teaching is first of all teaching a person. Somewhere along the line, someone had failed with Jane. Carryl Cope? That was Jane's own excuse and it would be dangerous indeed to jump to any such conclusion. Yet Lucy felt shaken. Was anyone safe from the perils of such responsibility? How carelessly she had criticized her own professors down the years! How little she had known or understood what tensions drove them on and tore them apart, what never-ending conflict they must weigh and balance each day. For she had come to see that it was possible, if one worked hard enough at it, to be prepared as far as subject matter went—though Lucy herself could not imagine such a blessed state—but it was not possible to be prepared to meet the twenty or more individuals of each class, each struggling to grow, each bringing into the room a different human background, each—Lucy felt now—in a state of peril where a too-rigorous demand or an instantaneous flash of anger might fatally turn the inner direction. Was she, for instance, shutting out Pippa's pleas for personal attention and response out of selfishness, fatigue, an unwillingness to give away anything of her inmost heart to a student? How did one know? How did one learn a sense of proportion, where to withdraw, where to yield?

And she guessed, not for the first time, that there could be no answer ever, that every teacher in relation to every single student must ask these questions over and over, and answer them differently in each instance, because the relationship is as various, as unpredictable as a love affair.

CHAPTER 8

Lucy woke to a dull dead gray November day with an icy wind whipping round the buildings. Everyone ran across the campus, driven like a few late leaves; mufflers were wound round necks; knees over long woolen socks looked blue. Pieces of newspaper rose and fell and were flattened against stone steps; everything had a desolate, naked air. If only it would snow, Lucy thought, as she put her head down against the wind and walked fast toward her freshman class. She had with her a briefcase full of terrible papers.

The room when she got there, panting after the three flights of stairs, had the stale smell of a winter room, overheated; she flung open a window, feeling impatient with and irritated by the two or three students who sat there, as passive as fish. Then, as the bell pealed out, shrill and startling no matter how hard one had listened for it, the others came thundering in, blowing on fingers, unwinding scarves, and Lucy experienced the tremor of anxiety that always accompanied this moment of suspense.

Was it the subdued giggle in the back of the room, when one of the new arrivals slammed the window shut again? Or was it the sullen expression of Mary Ford in the front row, she who was apt to explain accusingly that she had sat up all night over a paper that was marked D minus, as if tired work were a virtue and deserved a better grade? Something in the atmosphere touched Lucy like a whip. She brushed the notes she had been reading over aside, and stood up, hardly aware of the amount of suppressed emotion she was about to release.

"Wake up!" She was astonished to hear herself saying, "It's nine o'clock in the morning and you look like a drove of whales washed up by the tide."

Laughter rose and then quickly subsided as they sensed that this had not been meant kindly, or as a joke. They all shifted nervously, their eyes open very wide, like children at a play.

"Now listen!" Lucy opened *The Iliad* and began to read. She read as she had never managed to read before, the words falling like hailstones because she was so angry. And she could feel the electric current she was setting up, the something like a sigh that ran across the room and bound them together, those twenty-five wandering attentions, into a fused whole. She read here and there, sometimes giving a word of explanation to remind them of where the passage appeared; she read for twenty minutes by the clock that ticked relentlessly in front of her. Then, when she had finished and closed the book, she took three of the worst papers out and read a paragraph or two from each of them.

"This was the material before you, and this is how you honored it," she said, looking at the class with real hostility. "Here is one of the great mysterious works of man, as great and mysterious as a cathedral. And what did you do? You gave it so little of your real selves that you actually achieved boredom. You stood in Chartres cathedral *unmoved*. For the ancients this book was very much what a cathedral became for the people of the Middle Ages, a storehouse of myth, legend, and belief, the great structure where faith was nourished and the values of a civilization depicted . . . and you didn't bother to look at it!"

She picked up another of the dull C papers and read it through. "This is not a matter of grades. You'll slide through all right. It is not bad, it is just flat. It's the sheer poverty of your approach that is horrifying!"

Now for the first time Lucy heard the appalled silence she had created around her. The class seemed hardly to be breathing. But she was riding a wave, and had to go on as she had begun, until the wave broke, until the bell rang. "Very well," she ended. "Your next assignment is *Job*. Please come prepared to discuss it, and that means *think*."

The clock gave a final tick in the silence and then the bell shrilled out. At that moment the class, to Lucy's immense surprise, burst into spontaneous applause. She had been so concentrated that she had entirely forgotten herself and, in a curious way, even the class. Their applause made her blush.

"I'm sorry," she said, "but you deserved it."

As soon as the spell was broken, she realized that she had spoken as she did, with that violence, because Jane Seaman had been in the back of her mind all the time, Jane's kind of intensity; as if she had been so angry with these freshmen because they would never have the wit to discover Simone Weil's essay, let alone steal from it, as if her burst of rage had been an unconscious defense of Jane. Yes, she saw now, whatever had happened in her office the day before, she had committed herself to the defense.

"That was wonderful," a clear young voice broke into her thoughts. "Why didn't you get angry before?"

Lucy laughed, but underneath, and as she walked back across the campus, she felt humiliated. "No, no, no," she said aloud.

"No what?" It was, surprisingly enough, Jennifer Finch who stood there before her, smiling, "You seem to be saying a rather definite 'no' to the world at large."

"I've just put on an exhibition of rage to a class of Freshmen. Now I feel ashamed."

"Why?"

Faced with this question, Lucy had to think. "I suppose one has the idea that if one can only get their real attention by having a tantrum, one must be a rather poor teacher."

"Well . . ." Jennifer Finch lifted her chin and looked about, taking her time, as she always did. "Isn't it a matter of temperament? Maybe that is one way you can communicate; I would find it devastating, but I am not you."

"Oh *you* know," Lucy said fervently.

"I know plenty about failure, if that is what you mean."

So they all said, Lucy thought, recognizing the climate of this profession as one might recognize the climate of a nunnery, the daily, hourly examination of conscience.

"I suppose," she faltered, "there are as many kinds of good teachers as there are of artists."

"It is an art," Miss Finch responded, for once, instantly. And then with her usual unexpected slant, she added, "It is also an art to be a student. I wonder sometimes if we think enough about that. Learning is such a very painful business. It requires humility from people at an age where the natural habitat is arrogance," and she smiled her discreet smile. "But, oh dear me, here I am philosophizing when I should be teaching a class in calculus this minute."

Lucy watched her go, the stooped figure in a mackintosh, like an angel in the most inappropriate of disguises, and wondered if she knew about Jane yet, and if Carryl Cope knew. She felt reluctant to go back to her room, where she would have to decide whether to go home for Thanksgiving or not. On her desk lay a letter from her mother, and the question loomed. She was aware that she did not really want to go. She remembered hearing that if an animal is caged long enough it does not want to be released, and will not walk out through an open door. It had taken her all these weeks to get acclimatized to the cage of Appleton, and now she was almost afraid of a few days absence from it, of the whole adjustment to life at home (shades of John too), to her mother's moods, to the inevitable calls on her two aunts. What she longed to do was go off somewhere alone, to a hotel in a strange city, and there quietly chew the cud of these last weeks, ruminate, be still, read. . .

On an impulse she turned back and decided to visit Hallie's eleven o'clock class; perhaps the witnessing of a master of the art would help quiet her mind and set things back into a true balance again. At least it would keep her from facing everything on her desk for another hour.

"May I?" Lucy asked, at the door.

"Of course, delighted to have you." While the girls assembled, Hallie sat at her desk, with a pile of books before her, entirely concentrated on something she was reading. Lucy noticed the warmth of this room where the romantic poets and the English novel had been taught for so many years: pots of African violets on the window-sill, the worn torn map of the British Isles on the wall, posters of the Lake Country, of Bath, and the bookshelves at the back crammed with pamphlets and clippings. Hallie faced a semicircle of chairs three rows deep; this was a popular course. She did not lift her head until the bell had rung, until the girls were seated and quiet.

And Lucy herself felt the slight chill at her spine, the suspense, as the whole class was poised on silence. If this preparation had seemed to foretell a dramatic opening, a speech from the chair, the exact opposite took place. Hallie looked out the window a moment, then said quite casually,

"You have now all read at least some of the Keats letters. Would one of you like to read a passage aloud, or a whole letter that you think appropriate for class discussion?"

Half a dozen hands flew up, and they were launched.

It happened that the first two letters to be read aloud each spoke of "ripeness" or of "ripening," first an early one written in 1818: "Nothing is finer for the purpose of great productions than a very gradual ripening of the intellectual powers." (The last phrase, pointed up by Hallie in an ironic reference to themselves, caused a ripple of amusement.) The second and third choices introduced the Keats who educated himself by reading. "An extensive knowledge" (so he had written in May of 1818, so a young girl's voice repeated now) "is needful for thinking people—it takes away the heat and fever; and helps, by widening speculation, to ease the burden of Mystery . . ." They were familiar passages, of course, being rediscovered once more as if the ink were barely dry on the page. The students were excited (who would not be?). Lucy watched Hallie quietly pushing them to analyse, to bring together and consider as a whole the growth of this young man of genius, watched her do this with a casual question, with a smile of enjoyment, drawing attention to specific words, "a diligent indolence," or the pungent series of verbs from an early letter to Fanny, "go out and wither at tea parties; freeze at dinners; bake at dances; simmer at routs." For such a young man the evidence of pain might show itself first as irony. But Lucy sensed that Hallie was keeping tragedy at a distance still, deliberately holding the class back from the late feverish letters.

And slowly, what had been a painful, stumbling series of unrelated questions and answers became something like a fugue. Hallie was gently imposing a line, bringing them back to certain themes played over and over—thought, language, character, the making of a poet. And as she led the class back to these major chords, again and again, weaving in and out, asking the probing question, responding to the sensitive answer, what had in the first few moments been a professor "drawing out" a student, had become now a true dialogue. The students had been driven, probed, excited to a degree of concentration and power that could not have been imagined when the class began.

When Hallie finally recognized a girl who had waved her hand insistently all this while, it was clear that she had held this particular vision of the material in reserve, and that she launched it now, with a conscious sense of timing.

"We've talked and talked," the intense dark girl was wringing her hands with the relief of at last being allowed to speak, "but we haven't even approached what Keats was, nor what Fanny did to him!"

Half a dozen hands flew up in protest, and were quelled by a glance from Hallie, as the girl proceeded to read her evidence aloud, quoting first from that strong letter of 1819: "My mind is heap'd to the full; stuffed like a cricket ball—if I strive to fill it more it would burst. I know the generality of women would hate me for this; that I should have so unsoften'd, so hard a Mind as to forget them; forget the brightest realities for the dull imaginations of my own brain. But I conjure you to give it a fair thinking; and ask yourself whether 'tis not better to explain my feelings to you than to write an artificial Passion." This was followed by several examples from the searing letters a year later where illness and passion combined, as the girl said with a vehemence close to tears, to unman him. "You could not step or move an eyelid but it would shoot to my heart"; "I am sickened at the brute world which you are smiling with"; and she ended by stating that the proof of her thesis lay in the poems, where one could clearly see that all the great work preceded that last year, and heartless Fanny must be blamed, she who had fallen like a shadow even over the early letters: "Even as I leave off it seems to me that a few more moments thought of you would uncrystallize and dissolve me. I must not give way to it but turn to my writing again. If I fail I shall die hard."

As soon as she sat down, the argument began, a general clamor in which there was no thought of waiting for formal recognition. Lucy glanced at the clock. They had fifteen minutes to go against the brutal locking of the hour. Would Hallie herself never take over? For the eagerness, the excitement of discovery, the involvement that a first meeting with Keats must always elicit was there, but Lucy longed now for the voice of experience, for wisdom to shed its light at last. More than ever before she understood the marriage between a text and its reader. Keats himself was being diminished because these girls could only approach him with a thin layer of experience; the analysis of a text like this, she thought, is comparable to psychoanalysis. Everyone can get hold of a few simple formulas, but what knowledge, patience, and wisdom it must need to penetrate and fully understand the central complex of a personality!

"Let me bring this hour to a close by reading you three letters I have chosen," Hallie spoke at last. Her tone had changed. She laid aside the gentle questioner who had opened the door for each student into his own capacities for appreciation. The long-withheld summation was at hand. And the class, so sensitive an instrument in the hands of this teacher, felt it. Doodlers stopped doodling. There had been excitement; now the attention was of a different, more intense kind. Yet Hallie Summerson had not raised her voice, sat as she had sat all along, books open before her, glasses taken on and off nervously, a plain middle-aged woman in a shabby classroom. But now the reason for formal education became apparent. For what took place before Lucy's eyes was created by Hallie, but had been born in her because of the class before her, and sprang from all that had preceded it. Lucy had observed the whole process, the initial enthusiasm, the disciplining of this rather loose excitement, then the gentle artful playing of a fugue where they ceased to be master and pupil and became partners in the dialogue, and finally the launching of a brilliant student who might be counted on to take them to the heart. Out of all these together, the summation flowered.

Never, Lucy felt sure, would Hallie Summerson be able to speak to one person as she now did to sixty. Something streamed out of her that was absolutely open, passionate, of an intensity that made shivers go up and down Lucy's spine. It was the freeing of a *daimon,* as surely as the writing of a poem springs from the freeing of the poet's *daimon*. It surrounded Hallie Summerson with the aura of a person set apart, lonely and—Lucy half-smiled at the word, but uttered it to herself nevertheless—sacred.

Yet what she was actually doing seemed simple enough —the reading of three carefully chosen letters, followed by a brief analysis of the romantic point of view, its risks, its weakness, its tendency to surpass the reality of occasions and people and to create a dangerously intense world of its own: Keats and Fanny Brawne. But also its capacity to inspire works of art; a whole world of sensation, thought, passion at its most naked and suffering, built around the small figure of a woman, utterly unable to bear the burden laid upon her. "Alas, poor Fanny," Hallie said wryly, "Who can blame her? Life is not a Wagnerian opera and Fanny was asked to play a giant role."

The bell rang, shattering the moment like a shot breaking a glass. It was the measure of that moment that neither the class nor their professor paid the slightest heed. She read the Bright Star sonnet, closed the book, gathered up her papers, said, "Think it over—" and was gone before anyone stirred.

Lucy sat on alone, on the hard chair, after everyone else had gone, thinking it over. She felt sure that only from immense inner reserve, only from the secret life, the dedicated life, could such moments be created. They came from innocence, deep as a well, the innocence of those who have chosen to set themselves apart for a great purpose: "the teacher," a voice from a cloud. This power, Lucy suspected, had to be as carefully guarded as the creative power of the artist. What nourished it? Would she herself ever do more than stand at the threshold of the mystery, stand there with awe, but outside? Would she ever herself be a keeper of the sacred fire?

CHAPTER 9

When Lucy got back to her room just after lunch, she found a pencilled note on the hall table, marked urgent: Professor Cope asked her to drop in later on in the day. But urgencies faded before the first steady fall of snow. Lucy opened the window and knelt beside it, tasting the cool freshness, the stately, suspended, hypnotic fall, drank in the silence, and finally fell onto her bed as if she had been drugged, to sleep a dreamless sleep.

When she woke she could not remember where she was, started up in a panic, then feverishly pulled on overshoes, a woolen scarf, a raincoat, as excited and lifted up by the scene outside as she had always been as a child. If only her destination could have been Nowhere, some empty field where she could lean against a tree and watch the magic world being shaped around her. But as she stepped out and felt the gentle touch like a kitten's paw on her eyelids and mouth, she had to accept the fact that her destination was Carryl Cope. She stuffed her hands into her pockets and walked fast, head bent, thinking what a strange day this had been so far, a day of revelations, and dreading what new mysteries she would have to meet in a few moments. She had been summoned for what purpose? As whipping boy? Confidante? Or merely as a necessary source of information? It is idiotic, Lucy admonished herself, to be nervous. After all, Carryl Cope is not an ogre and I have done nothing wrong. Nevertheless, it was an effort to leave the gentle, gentling world of the snow outside, ring the bell, and climb that long black tunnel of stairs to the great blank door.

It opened, and Carryl Cope said shortly, "Ah, it's you. Thank goodness!" In the gray light of the library, she looked stern, a little forbidding. "I suppose I should thank you," she said drily, waving Lucy to an armchair. Then she launched at once into the subject at hand, as if she had been waiting so impatiently that she could not stop for the amenities. "It would have been a serious matter if we had not caught the issue of *Appleton Essays* in time."

"In time?" Lucy asked, bewildered.

"I spent the morning calling back every single number that had been sent out. Fortunately, only about forty in all. It was not officially for sale, you know. The students, at least, had not had a chance to get hold of it."

Lucy had come prepared for personal distress, possibly anger, but not to meet this administrator, concerned chiefly with the appearances of things, who stood, triumphant, her arms folded, leaning against the big desk.

"I feel very badly about the whole thing," Lucy said mechanically.

"No reason why you should. You're not responsible."

"I don't like being the messenger of evil tidings."

"Nobody does." But Lucy sensed that the gods were angry. Afraid of too long a pause, she floundered, "I suppose it will have to go to the student council."

"Those prigs! Not if I can help it!"

It was an astonishing answer. Did Carryl Cope imagine that she could circumvent the natural order of things?

"But can you help it?" she asked. "I thought . . ."

"You thought there were laws, but laws were made for man. My dear Lucy, we cannot afford to have a person of this quality blackballed for life, for that is what it would amount to. We have some human responsibility."

"I couldn't agree with you more," Lucy said fervently.

"Oh?" The eyes that had been so hard and fixed, softened. "Really? I thought you were out for blood."

"Why did you think that?"

"Because you're young. The young are frightfully self-righteous as a rule (you witnessed the vote about that irritating mathematical genius and saw how the instructors behaved); because you're new here and might feel undue respect for the powers that be . . . and because I gather you are not especially fond of Jane."

Lucy prickled. "I certainly recognize that she is not ordinary."

"Now don't be cross. I couldn't bear it." The raw nerve showed for the first time. "Let's sit down and talk about this calmly." But instead of sitting down, she walked to the windows and looked out. "Thank heavens, it's snowing," she murmured. "That wind nearly drove me crazy, making a shutter bang." She turned back, took a cigarette out of an alabaster box on the table, and looked down at Lucy. "You have had a talk with Jane, Hallie tells me . . ." Then she lit the cigarette and inhaled deeply.

"Yes." Lucy had known this was coming, known that she would have to meet it, but now she was thoroughly scared. How much could she afford to tell without betraying Jane? To whom was she responsible?

"What did she have to say for herself?"

The room appeared to Lucy to have grown immense in the last few seconds; the books in their tall bookcases towered over her; the weight of the moment seemed projected from the walls themselves while outside the incessant, silent falling whiteness made her feel she was inside a spell, as if she had been walking in a limbo for hours and longed only to be allowed to sleep. She put a hand up to her forehead.

"You're tired. I'm going to make you a cup of tea. I must admit that the last twenty-four hours have been rather a strain for everybody." The voice called back from down the hall, "Come and talk to me!"

Obediently Lucy rose and followed, and stood with her

back against the door frame while Carryl Cope puttered about absentmindedly with cups and saucers on a tray. It was clear that Lucy was being given a temporary reprieve. "I seem to remember your thinking that a college was a safe little world." For the first time the mischievous look had come back into the hooded eyes.

"Did I say that? It must have been a long time ago—"

"It's simply a microcosm where every normal instinct and emotion gets raised to the nth power."

"That doesn't seem quite sane."

"It's not. You need the guts of a camel to endure it." Lucy laughed.

"Well, *don't* you?"

"I got into a rage with my freshmen this morning . . ." Lucy felt the appraising probing eye upon her. "And you felt guilty, I suppose? Actually there's nothing as efficacious as a little *piqûre* of anger now and then. Gets their sluggish adrenal glands into action, don't you know?"

"I felt it was a failure."

"Nonsense. It's a costly method, costly to oneself, I mean. But it usually works. The strength one needs!" she said, lifting the tray and preceding Lucy back to the library. When she had set it down, she drew the curtains and turned on the lights. As Lucy took long swallows of tea, things seemed to have got back to their natural proportions.

"Now, shoot!" It was a command, though it was given with a smile. "What *did* Jane have to say?"

Because the atmosphere had changed, Lucy no longer felt any hesitation. She must tell Carryl Cope the truth, but as she began to talk she realized how baffled she still was by the exhausting scene with Jane, how little she really understood, and how very difficult if not impossible it was to try to sort out mere defensiveness from reality. But she could not turn back, and she did not spare Carryl Cope the impact of Jane's breakdown and her violent accusations about having been forced beyond her strength.

Carryl Cope listened in absolute silence, making no comment. Occasionally she sighed, a deep sigh, as unconscious as her gesture of pouring herself another cup of tea without offering one to Lucy.

"It does seem to me," Lucy ended, "that severe punishment at this point would solve nothing."

"She has been punished enough." There followed a long silence. Lucy had the feeling that Carryl Cope had forgotten she was there. She seemed very remote, lost literally, in thought. When she spoke, her face had no expression except one of immense fatigue and distaste. "Of course the dreadful fact is that one loses trust. How many of Jane's other performances were borrowed? Must we track it all down, check and recheck every single thing we have ever published of hers? It makes me feel sick."

"You must talk to her yourself."

"Of course." Carryl Cope got up and began to pace up and down the room, slowly. "Good Christ!" The swearword was like a cry of anguish. "I suppose what this girl

needs is a psychiatrist. That's what you think, isn't it?"
She turned back to Lucy fiercely.

"Maybe."

"I've given her everything I had to give, hours of time—
she came here when she chose. What more could I have
given?" she asked sitting down again.

"I don't know," Lucy said miserably. "Only perhaps
you gave a great deal to the mind, but something got left
out that would have made it right. Somehow she got
twisted up. Somehow she felt deprived. The heart . . ."

"Mind? Heart?" Carryl Cope refused to accept or perhaps did not hear what Lucy had, trembling, implied. She
got up, pacing again back and forth down the big room,
thinking aloud. "Good work is done when these two move
in harness. Jane was not just a brilliant mind." (Lucy
winced at the use of the past tense.) "She had that extra
dimension of passionate interest. I didn't feel I was pushing her; she asked for it, bombarded my door for books."
(But what was she really after, Lucy wondered, not books,
possibly not books at all.) "You know, Lucy," Carryl Cope
bore down again, demanding her full attention, "students
don't do that every day. It is, I suppose, intoxicating. It's
like watching bamboo grow a yard a night, or whatever
it does. I have never found teaching a drudgery, but I
must admit that one does a good deal of lifting the stodgy
or the paralysed over the years—here was someone who
could run!"

Lucy nodded in silence. Her mind was racing, but there

was nothing that she dared to say. Suffering, bafflement filled the room.

"Also," Carryl Cope stood still for a moment, "she was lonely, as the brilliant always are. I had the illusion that she found something just by being here, an atmosphere where she could breathe, her natural element. There were times last year when she came and spent half a day in this room, just reading while I worked." She glanced round the walls with a cold eye, then sat down suddenly, and asked in an ironic voice that could not conceal pain, "Where did I go wrong? What happened? Am I crazy to think that for Jane Seaman to behave as a thief is a personal attack; that, consciously or not, it is an attack on me?"

Lucy froze. What did one answer?

"Well!"

"I don't know," Lucy said. "I think perhaps it was. But I don't know," she repeated, too aware of the gap between them, the years, the rank, the fact that however much compassion she might feel for Carryl Cope, it was not her place to dispense it.

"You are somewhere between me and Jane in age." The voice seemed to have penetrated Lucy's thoughts. "You are sufficiently detached. I am asking you to be honest with me. Take it as a compliment, if you wish." Such an appeal had to be answered.

"Jane said it was like taking jumps on a horse with the bars set higher and higher. My guess is that at some point she went into panic. Possibly she realized without really knowing it that something was being left out; perhaps she wanted something of you quite desperately that you could not afford to give. It's not that she was right, only that she was stuffing herself with the wrong food and suffering from malnutrition, if you like." Lucy had never felt more inept in her life, nor less capable of playing the curious role assigned to her by sheer chance, that of judging two people whom she hardly knew, and their relationship which she came to in abysmal ignorance.

Carryl Cope gave a deep sigh. It was her only response. Then she suddenly lifted her head. "I simply won't accept giving up now!" Strength, which had seemed to ebb from the bent figure a few moments before, flowed back with such force that Lucy was startled. It was as if a barren winter tree, battered, with half its trunk gone, had suddenly leafed over. "I'm not going to give Jane up. If, at least in my own heart, I accept it as my failure not hers (and you almost persuade me, you perspicacious child!), then she may still come out all right, graduate, go on. If"—and she paused while her eyes flashed out on Lucy like a hawk's—"if the thing can be hushed up. I'm going to fight, Lucy!"

"There is still Jane's point of view," Lucy said, too aware of the prickly path Carryl Cope was setting out on. "You will meet resistance."

"After all, I'm saving her skin!"

"People are not necessarily grateful for that."

"Aren't they? Why not?" The fire, the teasing stance had come back.

Lucy took a deep breath. This was it. "Part of Jane wants to fail is my guess, wants to commit suicide, if you will. Part of her wants to be punished. Don't you see, if she comes out of this without paying the price, she will have to face the burden of her brilliance again—and your expectations of it."

But once more Carryl Cope brushed a suggestion aside as irrelevant to the current she was on. There was something splendid in this will, splendid and tragic. Had Carryl Cope ever for one instant really put herself in Jane's shoes?

"I'm staking all I've got on Jane."

"That's rather grand," said Lucy.

"Making a dreadful mess I'm doing my best to cover up? Nothing very grand about me, I'm afraid. An hour ago I thought I would resign."

"You take it that seriously?" Lucy was again taken by surprise by this astonishing woman.

"Send Jane Seaman to a psychiatrist and resign!"

"They would seem to you an equal admission of failure, I suppose?" and Lucy could not help smiling.

"Naturally. Teachers who abandon their students to psychiatrists had better resign, by my books."

Once more the power of indomitable innocence struck Lucy hard. But she guessed—and with dread—that Carryl Cope would need every weapon she could muster to sustain it in the weeks to come.

"If I can be of any help, as time goes on—" she said, getting up to leave.

"I consider you a friend, Lucy. I count on you."

"I am honored." The word was formal.

"Pish tush! I'm a silly old fool and you know it." But at the door, she frowned, looked at Lucy a shade anxiously as she said, "I'll see Jane this evening. Meanwhile I need not insist that the utmost discretion is in order."

"Hallie knows. I think no one else does."

"Good gracious, child! I'd forgotten about the snow. Will you be all right?" Carryl Cope pulled the long string of the hall light, as if to make sure that Lucy was properly dressed.

"I love the snow," Lucy said.

But she hardly noticed it, as a matter of fact, walking with her head bent and asking herself a series of questions with no possible answers at present. What is really being defended? Jane Seaman? Carryl Cope? A point of view about intellectual brilliance divorced from life that must be maintained or too much would crumble? And what is justice, Lucy asked herself, for she felt at the moment that justice was cruel, cruel to everyone in this case. Yet can justice be laid aside so lightly? What is justice? She asked the whirling snow. The answer was a gust of wind that made her shiver and turn up her coat collar.

CHAPTER 10

This time there was to be no faculty meeting, and no meeting of the student council. Lucy thought a little wryly that this time the messenger with evil tidings had delivered his message not to a temporal king who would have received it in public, but to one of the jealous, personal, all-powerful gods. Jane came to class, as imperturbably in control of herself, apparently, as before. A simple statement made its appearance on the bulletin boards, apologizing for an unforeseen delay in the publication of the fall issue of *Appleton Essays*. On the surface everything seemed settled.

Under the surface, however, rumor and gossip flourished. Twice Lucy had the feeling when she walked into a group of fellow instructors at the Club that her entrance brought on a quick change of subject. She was in a situation where frankness was impossible, and the necessity to be discreet meant in effect that she must keep away from *the* subject altogether; all this tried her nature. The only person she could talk to was Hallie, but even Hallie had seemed lately to have withdrawn. She had told Lucy that Carryl had not only had the promised talk with Jane, but also with the President, and things had been satisfactorily hushed up, if that was the word to use for this universal buzz that never came out into the open.

"Carryl is taking a long chance," she said at the end of a rather stiff tea.

"She is defending what she believes in," Lucy had answered, torn between loyalties, "and what she believes in is rather grand."

"Yes, of course." But the slow blush—was it shame? anger?—that followed on this instantaneous response seemed to deny it.

They had left it at that.

The snow had melted fast, but something of the excitement of winter stayed on, the air clear and brilliant, the ring of a heel on frosty pavement, a peculiar evening light when the white houses seemed to be floating on the violet air and dark fell like a curtain before one knew it. And, in spite of the prickly situation around Jane, Lucy was often flooded with happiness so fresh and overwhelming that she began to believe that teaching might be her vocation after all. The freshman section had roused itself after her outburst of anger: three of the girls had written good papers on *Job* and the class discussion had been heated, one of those hours when Lucy felt she was not so much teaching as witnessing a group of intelligent girls teach themselves. She would never have thought this particular section capable of fervor. But she suspected that the subject matter had something to do with it; *Job* touched them at crucial points in their own experience; religion was a subject they wrestled with outside the curriculum, no doubt. It occurred to her that it was perhaps only at points of conflict that some door in the lazy attention was finally forced open, and people became educable—at least if the conflict were not too intense or deeply buried, she reminded herself, thinking of Jane. She was absorbed in these thoughts and smoking a cigarette before putting her mind on reading and correcting a long paper, when a knock roused her, a tentative knock.

"Come in," she called. "Oh, come in, Pippa."

"I brought my paper," Pippa said, "I couldn't wait."

"Good," Lucy smiled. "I'm looking forward to reading it." Instinctively she went back to sit down at her desk. "Well, Pippa," she said kindly, "how are things with you?"

She was struck by the open beauty of the face before her, wrapped in a blue muffler which Pippa had twisted round her neck and over her head so that it framed the purity of line, the long oval. For just a second Lucy felt a pang at the passing of youth. Life had seemed to her rich a moment before, but it was passing, passing . . .

"You'd better take off your coat and sit down. How is it out?"

"Cold and starry." Pippa sat down on the bed, beside her coat, one hand rubbing the dark-blue wool absent-mindedly.

"There's something on your mind, child. What is it?" How revolting to say "child"! It had slipped out, setting Pippa outside, making her feel that her problem, whatever it was, must be a childish one. Here it all is again, Lucy groaned inwardly, conflict, self-criticism. Here we go again!

"You said if I ever had a real problem I could come." As usual those large eyes had filled with tears, and Lucy felt wildly impatient. She waited while Pippa apparently measured the leap she was about to take. The image came to Lucy's mind of herself as a child crouching before the broad jump, measuring it with her eyes, waiting for the moment when she would have the courage to force her heavy weight through the air, feel the knees release from the tense spring in them—and she smiled.

"It's serious," Pippa said a little defiantly. "It's about Jane."

"Oh?" Lucy froze. "What about Jane? Jane seems to be managing very well."

"That's just it. I mean, no one can understand. Of course we all know about the *Iliad* essay. You can't expect such things to get completely hushed up on this campus!"

"No, I expect not."

"Miss Winter, I am not a member of student government, but my roommate is." There was a pause. Apparently Pippa now lacked the courage to take the jump.

"She feels that student government should have been brought in, no doubt."

"Yes, she does. They criticize you, and Professor Cope. I couldn't stand it any longer. Oh, Miss Winter, why has it been hushed up? It seems so *unfair*. No one understands."

"You know," Lucy paused to light a cigarette, "this is not a very simple question, Pippa."

"But Jane *did* plagiarize!"

"Yes, she did." It was an impasse, and Lucy found it impossible to say more.

"They say it's a pure case of favoritism; if anyone else had done what Jane did, they would have been expelled."

"I can believe that's what they say. But, you know Pippa, sometimes one has to ignore what 'they say.'"

"It's not good when the students distrust the faculty," Pippa said with vehemence. "It's horrible. I hate it all!" She began to cry.

Lucy felt stiff and sore; Pippa's tears, this time, could not be pushed aside as self-indulgent, but she could find no word of consolation to speak.

"I don't understand," Pippa sobbed. "I don't understand any of it. Why should Jane get away with this? Why?"

"The punishment is so severe that it would mean the

end of her education. Is the image of justice worth that? Don't you think what she has to bear from having been exposed and from her own conscience is punishment? Should we snarl, rush at her, and tear her limb from limb because this is the rule of the tribe? Honestly, Pippa!"

"She doesn't seem to be suffering at all. She's triumphant!" Pippa had stopped crying. She was simply very angry. "It's not fair to have a student council if, when something like this happens, they are not allowed to exercise their power. It's undemocratic!" It came out with the false emphasis of someone who is repeating phrases she has heard.

"Oh democracy, the crimes that are committed in thy name!"

But suddenly Lucy met Pippa's honest gaze and felt ashamed. "You mustn't let me down."

"I'm sorry. I am just not in a position to say very much."

But this was a mistake, as Pippa's quick response made clear. "Of course everyone knows it's Professor Cope. Jane has always been her pet."

This was something Lucy could not evade. "I would like to say one thing about Jane: whatever she did and for whatever stupid reasons or non-reasons, she *is* a brilliant student. This is not a case of a poor student trying to get by. Surely, Pippa, Jane is worth saving?"

"Oh, she's bright enough. But does that excuse a criminal? Do people who steal get let off because they're brilliant? You yourself said that stealing ideas was worse than stealing money!"

"I know," Lucy said, miserably confused by this voice that insisted on saying aloud all her own doubts.

"You don't agree with Carryl Cope. You can't!"

"Well, I must admit that I am not sure what I think." Lucy was abysmally aware of that. She was only making things worse every time she opened her mouth.

"It ought to come out into the open. It's bad for the college, all this whispering in corners. Do you think it helps Jane? No one speaks to her. She's an absolute pariah!"

"Is she?" This was news to Lucy. "Isn't there any faction on her side? Hasn't she talked to any of you about it?"

"She's never talked to us," Pippa said bitterly. "Her roommate says she's never even cried."

But now Lucy sat up straight and had something to say. "It takes some courage to face out the self-righteous indignation of your peers. My sympathy is with Jane."

"I can't believe it," Pippa said with dignity. "I just can't believe it," she repeated, outrage written on her face.

"Well," Lucy smiled, "you'll find out in time that you come to believe a lot of things you once said you couldn't believe."

"Gosh, I think you're wonderful!" The radiant aura of love, spoken at last, surrounded Pippa and made Lucy flush. She had no idea why this sudden reversal from indignation to passionate approval, but it was certainly a relief.

"I feel like a perfect ass," Lucy said.

And suddenly they both laughed. "Well, no one else admits it. One thing that enrages us is the solid smug front the faculty presents—as if there were a wall between us and them. You don't do that. You admit that you are confused."

"Oh dear," Lucy sighed, and lit a cigarette. She found undeserved praise sweet; she was grateful to Pippa, grateful for the trust that had given her courage to take the leap, after all. "It was good of you to come and talk to me, Pippa. But please remember that I am inexperienced and if I have doubts, they spring partly from lack of wisdom. I want you to know that I have the greatest respect for Professor Cope."

"Please try to explain," Pippa said, her eyes shining.

The walls have fallen, Lucy thought, moved in spite of herself. For she sensed that the intimacy which this painful interview was establishing between her and Pippa, far from feeding a "crush" as she had feared it would, was rooted now in mutual respect. "How are they to learn anything about feeling if they don't feel?" she heard Carryl Cope asking.

"When a student as brilliant as Jane does something so fantastically out of character as to steal a paper, and risk having it published to boot, what do you suppose motivates her?"

"I don't know," Pippa wailed.

"Well, think. Here is a girl who has borne the full weight of belief, who has been constantly spurred by a tremendously powerful personality. Has it ever occurred to you that being 'teacher's pet,' as you call it, may be a very demanding role to play? It's possible that Jane couldn't stand the strain this apparently fortunate relationship imposed. I have even imagined—this is pure guesswork—that she stole the essay with the unconscious hope that she would be discovered and so set free." Lucy felt the weight of Pippa's concentrated attention now and trembled. What if she were wrong? "I have to trust you, Pippa, now. Don't you think that if you were Professor Cope and realized that you had laid a heavy burden on a very young person, had forced her perhaps beyond her strength, that you would wish to take the blame? And if you assumed that responsibility—surely not an ignoble act—would it not be a responsibility toward true justice, not just the pattern of custom or law? Would it be just to punish someone who, instead of punishment, was in dire need of help?"

While she spoke, Lucy had felt forced to get up, to move around. Now she stood opposite Pippa and gently laid a hand on the bent head.

"You make me ashamed," Pippa said.

"I don't mean to. I've only tried to let you through the wall onto the other side." And then, feeling that the atmosphere had been highly charged long enough, she added with a smile, "Maybe now you can take the mes-

sage to Garcia—it *is* rather a jungle world you have to
penetrate."

"I wish you would talk to the student council," Pippa
said feverently. "I wish you would!"

"I'm sorry, but that would be to assume a function
beyond my scope. Why don't you suggest to your roommate that she take the matter up with the President?
That might help clear the air."

"Yes," Pippa sighed. "Oh, I feel so much better," she
added. "You can't imagine."

"I feel better, too," Lucy admitted. "You're a good
girl, Pippa."

At the door they shook hands warmly . . . like two
human beings for a change, Lucy thought. And not for
the first time that day, she caught herself wondering
whether crisis may be one of the climates where education flourishes—a climate that forces honesty out, breaks
down the walls of what ough to be, and reveals what *is*,
instead.

CHAPTER 11

On the Tuesday before the Thanksgiving break there was already departure in the air, as the clotted unity of the college became atomized into four or five hundred individuals each with a separate destination. Holidays, Lucy sensed, were dangerous; the careful threading together of each class, the continuity, all that had been built up day by day was shifting and would suddenly break apart. But if holidays were dangerous, they were also necessary, and especially this holiday which might divert the underground flow and discontent of spirit in which the college as a whole found itself.

Debby, inviting Lucy over for cocktails, had said, "We all need a drink!" and Lucy had heartily agreed. Now she enjoyed putting on a red dress, looking at herself in the mirror, a woman about to go forth and talk with her contemporaries for a change. It was a relief to saunter across campus, letting the reins she held so tightly slacken a little and tasting the slightly acid smell of the day, overcast but not cold, as if it were a cordial. I'm happy, she thought; in spite of everything, I'm happy. It was that pure happiness she recognized as a friend, happiness that comes from nowhere, for no reason, like a flash of sunlight, happiness made of nothing, a red dress, a party. Debby, who was outdoors raking leaves in the yard, waved. "I'll be right with you! Walk in . . ."

The Atwoods had painted the walls themselves, pale gray, streaked in spots, and Henry had put up shelves, long planks, with bricks for ends to hold some of the books; others were still piled on the floor; the furniture was a mixture of wicker garden furniture and shabby Victorian which they had no doubt picked up around Appleton; there was a bunch of chrysanthemums in a tall tin can. Lucy smiled as she noticed Henry's initials, wreathed in flowers, painted upon it.

"What a lot you've done, Debby!"

By the time the Beveridges arrived, bringing Jennifer Finch with them in their car, Henry had mixed a martini, and they settled in, whispering and cheeping, chattering and whistling like a flock of birds, as if they had not seen each other for years. They talked about colors for the room—Debby was still looking for curtain material—

about the latest novels, about how much a really good stereo setup would cost.

"What a holiday feeling!" Lucy exclaimed, slipping off one shoe,

"You're going home?" Miss Finch asked, a twinkle in her eye.

"Oh yes," Lucy sighed, deflated by the prospect. "It's rather dreary, as a matter of fact. Don't let's talk about that. I envy you people who really *live* here." She turned to Henry. "Isn't it fun to be settling in, making the bookshelves, raking your own leaves?"

Earnestly shining, he agreed that it was.

Maria was sitting on the floor, her legs stretched out before her, ankles crossed. "All I dream of is getting away to some warm place, of going to Italy, with all the children swarming in the back of the car."

"Italy in November can hardly be called warm," Jack said imperturbably. "This is the season when your Italian friends dream about central heating, an apartment house in New York with low ceilings and no draughts."

"Italy is warm to me at any season," Maria answered shortly.

"Carryl's going over this summer, the lucky dog!" Jack's had been an innocent enough remark, but Lucy felt the tension gather at once. The sentence lay on the air while they all sniffed at it, and walked around it, their hackles rising.

"I don't care," Maria burst out, "we've got to talk about it!"

"Do we have to, honey?" Jack murmured, but clearly without hope.

"I want to know what Jennifer thinks; the golden opportunity has arrived." Maria was half laughing but the smouldering look had come back into her eyes.

"I too yearn to know," Lucy said, turning toward Jennifer.

Jennifer sipped her drink as if she were considering it judicially, comparing it to other martinis, comparing this occasion to other occasions when martinis had been judged too dry or not quite dry enough. "I have an idea that the subject has become, for some occult reason, taboo."

"It's gone underground to poison the roots," Maria announced dramatically. "We all know that."

"There are times when I think Maria missed her vocation." Jack, Lucy thought, was still trying to keep things from going the way they certainly would go, willy-nilly, at this point. "She should have been a tragic actress trouping round the world playing Medea!"

Debby and Henry exchanged a look of amusement and pleasure. They were immensely likable, yet Lucy sometimes thought they were a little like chameleons, always hoping to find the background against which they might rest and stay the same color. Would Appleton be it?

"But perhaps Maria is right," Jennifer Finch remarked into the air. "Henry, let me congratulate you upon this martini. I pronounce it perfect." There she sat, a purple velvet bow at her throat, a fine voile blouse under her lavender tweed, her face crumpled and dear as a pansy's, enjoying the moment and even its tension to the full, unwilling to take anything whatever with morbid seriousness. She addressed herself to Jack, "Can you remember any event on this campus in any way comparable to this, or creating around it the atmosphere of the last weeks? I must confess that I cannot. It would be foolish to pretend we are not disturbed: we are."

"You've said it!" Jack answered with one of his lightning smiles.

"All I know," Debby said, "is that someone stole a piece that was to come out in *Appleton Essays*. All I know is that all copies have been withdrawn and this has created a huge buzz."

Jennifer Finch gave a sudden laugh, and then when she had thoroughly tasted her own amusement, laid it aside, and began to recite, "Teach me to heare Mermaids singing / Or to keep off envies stinging / and finde what winde / serves to advance an honest minde." This recitation was followed by a deep sigh. "What wind serves to advance an honest mind?" she asked them.

"We attended a faculty meeting not long ago at which the main theme was, you may remember, 'the price of excellence.'" Jack's tone was light. The woman is a genius, Lucy thought, for she was aware that Jennifer commanded the tone. "I suppose one might say of Carryl, bless her, that she is paying the price with a vengeance."

"Whose excellence, her own or that of Jane Seaman?" Maria was not going to be quelled.

"Possibly both. Wouldn't you agree?" Jack turned to Jennifer again. "Wouldn't you say that Carryl in this instance is defending herself *and* Jane?"

"I would so much like to be pinned down, or rather to pin myself down, but the more I look at all sides of this, the less I seem able to make up my mind what is right, what is wrong, or rather what is possible and what is impossible, right *or* wrong. One might at times decide that Carryl may be right, but what she has done, impossible."

"You reduce ethics to expediency, then?" Lucy asked.

"I am not quite ready to answer that cogent question." Jennifer smiled her slow smile.

"But how can it be right to cover up a crime?" Debby cried out.

"First of all we would have to decide who had committed the crime, and then just what the crime was."

"Yes!" Maria broke in triumphantly. "Yes, Jennifer, and the only possible explanation is that Carryl Cope herself feels guilty, and also that she is protecting an investment. She just can't admit that she has failed with Jane, failed abysmally, that the ugly duckling will never be a swan."

"But why is that a crime?" Lucy asked. "I mean, is one never allowed to make a mistake in this sacred grove?"

Jack riposted at the same instant, so their voices mingled. "Maybe Jane will turn out to be a swan! Carryl is betting heavily on *that*, it seems to me!"

"Whereas," Henry nodded eagerly, "Jane would be finished if she were expelled. And one hears that her family is no help. I feel sorry for her," he added, rather shame-facedly. "One might say about Jane, too, is one never allowed to make a mistake?"

"Some mistakes are irrevocable." Maria was flushed with anger. "For some mistakes you have to pay."

"You see what I mean about Medea? Relentless woman!" There was now a flicker of real hostility in Jack's tone.

It was Jennifer once more who slipped gently into the breach. "Things are complicated by the unfortunate fact that Jane is not loved—admired, perhaps—not loved. I'm afraid she has aroused envy and there seems to be an ineradicable streak in human nature that enjoys the fall of the mighty. Carryl herself is not immune." Again she sighed. "So we return by all these paths to the theme Jack suggested to be the key: the price of excellence. Odd that in one semester we should be faced with two such differ-ent examples of the same problem! Perhaps," she ended with an ironic smile, "we are being tried for some purpose we wot not of."

"Henry, get us another drink!" Debby came in now with a tray of pizza, and olives.

"Yes, if our spirits are to be tried, let us try them in the most favorable circumstances possible!" Henry disap-peared into the kitchen where he could be heard whistling and clattering ice cubes.

Jennifer continued to spin out her monologue. "The trouble is, of course, that the college may be represented *in essence* by Carryl Cope and Jane Seaman, the most brilliant of professors and the most brilliant of students, locked in what must seem to them a private struggle, but the fact remains that the college is a community . . ."

"Of course," Maria interrupted brusquely. "The students are in an uproar; so are the faculty. There has been no peace in our household since this damn thing happened." Lucy caught the misery as well as the anger here for the first time. It had evidently become a real war between Jack and Maria, and they were both suffering.

"So my point: what Carryl has chosen to do may be right, but it is not *possible*, was perhaps not too far from the mark, after all."

"Darling Jennifer, you are always right," Maria said warmly. It was evident that she was close to tears.

"Heavens, I trust not! That would make me quite impossible, wouldn't it?"

"If all this is so," Debby said, "what's going to happen next? I had no idea of all that could be involved in what seemed a simple case of plagiarism!"

"At some point," Lucy said, "some clarification will have to take place. It can't be avoided, can it, Professor Finch?"

"Jennifer, please! I hate being 'professored'; the mantle falls and the role must be played. This is a holiday from all our roles!" Her face had grown quite pink. "I cannot tell you what is going to happen. I wish I knew!"

"It could all simmer down, I suppose," Lucy said without conviction.

"Not likely!" Maria said. "Not without some catharsis."

Jennifer smiled. "The terms of Greek tragedy may seem slightly exaggerated, but on the other hand, they may not.

I would be inclined to fear that there will be an explosion."

"Jane might break down, for one thing," Lucy said. "She is, from what I gather, being ostracized by the students. Like Henry I can only say that I feel desperately sorry for her."

"Yes . . ." Jennifer put her hands to her forehead, pressing them against it as if she too were feeling the strain. "Yes . . ."

For the moment, they had reached the end of what there was to say. And everyone, no doubt, felt as Lucy did, exhausted by the complexity, longing only to be relieved of having to consider it for another moment. Would it be possible to change the subject? It was rather like a toothache; they had to keep feeling round the tooth, trying to diagnose the pain.

"How do you know Jane has been ostracized?" Maria asked Lucy. "From what I hear she goes around as if nothing had happened, her nose in the air!"

"We hear so many things . . ." Jennifer murmured.

"One of my students came to me to tell me she and her friends felt that the student council was being emasculated."

"Naturally!" Maria snorted. "Of course!"

"Whew, that was a tough nut to crack. How did you crack it?" Jack asked with the greatest interest. "If I am not being indiscreet, or merely intoxicated?"

"I told her that the council should call on the President and present their case to him . . . and I tried to make her see the other side, Carryl's side, a little. Was that wrong, I wonder?"

"You see!" Maria said triumphantly. "The most natural human relationships are being poisoned at the roots, just as I said. A professor hesitates to be honest with a troubled student who asks for help. Is this education?" She rose clumsily to her feet, to stand like an alarming slightly-larger-than-life-size goddess, and glared at them all.

"Poor Blake," Jack murmured to himself. "When the whole business stinks like a piece of rotten meat in a garbage can, when the maggots are at it, it will finally reach him, and he will have to deal with it."

"My guess is," Jennifer said quietly, "that Blake knows pretty well what is going on. Blake is no fool. I don't suppose any of you were in chapel yesterday, but I was—Blake chose to speak on the text 'O sancta simplicitas!' Jane is hardly a saint, but still some of those who were so eagerly bringing faggots to the fire may have stopped to think twice."

"Good old Blake!" Jack gave a shout of happy laughter. "Occasionally the Unitarian Minister comes out in a rush, I almost said 'rash.' So he, at least, is on the side of the angels," he said, chuckling again, and giving Maria a teasing glance.

"Your angel, maybe, not mine," she said bitterly. "No doubt Carryl Cope had a little talk with him."

Henry came back from the kitchen with a new supply of martinis just as Lucy caught Jack's look of icy dislike of his wife.

"Maria," he said. "It is time we went home. Thank you, Henry, but we really must leave this pleasant gathering before the explosion we have foretold happens right here."

"Ah!" Maria said, her eyes blazing. "He is angry. *At last*, he is angry!"

"Shut up, Maria!" Jack pushed her roughly toward the door. The gesture, so violent for him, was shocking.

"I won't be pushed out!" Maria cried, struggling. For a second it looked as if they might fall.

"Don't you think," Jennifer dominated them without raising her voice and without moving, "we might all sit down and try to achieve a calmer climate before we part? 'Teach me to heare, Mermaides singing, Or to keep off envies stinging. . . .' Do sit down, Jack dear. We cannot let you go in anger."

She was irresistible enough to stop the lightning as it flashed out. And Lucy longed to ask, What is your power, you so detached, you so gentle, you so subtly intelligent, you spinster held in thrall by your mother, yet, to us, safety and a continuous act of grace, the refuge of every one of our tormented minds—what is your power? But though the martinis might bring out hostility in the most reserved of men, they did not loosen the social bonds to the point where such deep feeling could be spoken.

Jack sat down again, so did Maria. But Lucy was dismayed to see that tears poured down from those defiant eyes; the most natural person among them was weeping uncontrollably.

"It is h–h–hell," she said. "Henry, give me another drink!"

"Your wish is my command," Henry said, arriving with his jug like a messenger a little too late with his message.

"Only, I have lost my glass."

"Maria, darling, please . . ." Jack handed his wife a new glass with a gesture as gentle and loving as his earlier one had been brutal.

"I feel mildly intoxicated," Jennifer announced, "a state my mother will not condone, and quite rightly. But it is a state that moves me to speak of Carryl. Our dear and noble Maria is suffering before our eyes, and may not this suffering spring in part from a—perhaps—I do feel tentative here—partial understanding of what Carryl Cope *is*, as a human being. And how she has become what she is? Am I speaking out of turn?" She turned to Jack with a luminous smile.

"Please go on," he said.

"I simply hate her." Maria spoke thickly through her tears.

"Yet you do not inhabit opposite poles of the universe of the soul. You have a great deal in common, you know."

"I—and Carryl Cope!" The tone was pure disdain.

"You and Carryl Cope. I read you, Maria, though perhaps I am—as they say—crazy, as an undisciplined passionate nature. In this occasionally fossilized atmosphere, you burn like a great exploding star. We are grateful. Carryl Cope is also a passionate nature, only one that has been severely disciplined."

"She has always had things her own way," said Maria, not softened.

"This is a small puddle and she is a big frog in it," Jennifer granted with one of her swallowed smiles. "But how is this kind of power achieved, would you guess?"

"By being Olive Hunt's pet, for one thing."

"No, Maria!" Jack flushed a furious red.

"Maria is only saying aloud what a great many people think, Jack. Please let me go on to the end of these probably irrelevant remarks."

"By all means."

"Are you aware that Carryl is one of perhaps five living historians of the pre-Renaissance who amounts to anything? Do you know, Maria, for instance, that she has been translated into Persian, Arabic, Japanese? If she had been a man instead of a woman. . ."

"As she obviously should have been," Debby broke in.

"That is possible. If she had been, there is no doubt that she would have been given the Haskins Chair at Harvard. Ten years ago Carryl faced the fact that she would stay here."

"At Harvard she would have been one of many big frogs —it might have taught her not to be so arrogant," Maria challenged.

Lucy had listened with increasing nervousness; the air was becoming too charged for Jennifer's subtle means to subdue, and she felt forced now to commit herself, to take a stand. "I must say I don't see the arrogance. She is a dedicated teacher, one senses, and it must be rather rare to find someone who can command two fields as she does. I suppose it must have caused her considerable conflict, one way and another. But why do people feel so bitterly about Olive Hunt? Why do you?" She turned to Maria now. "I should have thought this was a private matter."

For once Jennifer launched into speech without a second's hesitation. "Whatever Olive has done for Carryl has been repaid in full. Olive is an old woman now and it is she who has become dependent and demanding."

"Besides," Jack said with icy emphasis, "it happens to be a real relationship. The fact is that they love each other and have done so for twenty years. Beyond our recognition of that fact, I quite agree with Lucy, it is none of our damned business."

"Well," the adamant Maria pursued her course, "the question was, where does she get her power? You can't tell me that Olive Hunt's money has nothing to do with it— or that in the case of Jane Seaman the fact that Olive can choose to leave her money elsewhere may have influenced 'poor Blake,' as you call him."

There was a second's pause when they all realized that even Jennifer was powerless to prevent the explosion.

"What you need," Jack said, getting up violently, "is a good spanking!"

"If so, you are hardly the man to administer it."

The moment was so naked and painful that Lucy did not know where to look. Jennifer rose to her feet. "Perhaps it is time we retired to our separate lairs," she said. "I do not think, dear Jack, that Maria needs a spanking. She is too unhappy."

A great sob burst from the recumbent figure at her back. "Don't leave us, Jennifer. Don't go. . ."

"My dear, my mother is now in the middle of writing down in her still-elegant hand a prepared speech of re-crimination which she will deliver when I get back over half an hour later than I had promised."

"Not really?" Lucy found this statement nearly impossible to believe. "Are you serious, Jennifer?"

"Perfectly serious. Come, Jack, take me home, will you? You can come back and pick Maria up later. . ."

When they had left, the room looked disorganized as if the focussing center had fallen away. Debby got up and began to empty ashtrays and take the dirty glasses out. Henry, who had been very quiet, sat down and looked nervously at Maria, who was blowing her nose in silent withdrawal and grief.

"However did Jennifer Finch become what she is?" Lucy mused aloud, more to herself than to anyone else.

"Some people are born wise, I guess," Henry said.

"No one is born wise," Maria sat up. "What she must have endured from that dreadful old woman, I cannot imagine!"

"But there must be *something*," Lucy said, glad they had stumbled on a change of subject, "some redeeming quality . . ."

Maria's eyes were flashing again. "Let me give you an instance of what Mrs. Finch is like: she is arthritic, you know, and eats like a pig so she is very heavy. Last year she fell, and Jennifer had to call the police to help lift her into bed—it was late at night. Naturally Jennifer was anxious and got up several times to see that her mother was all right. So when, the next morning, Mrs. Finch announced that she had not slept a wink, Jennifer made the mistake of telling her that she had looked in once or twice and found her fast asleep. At this, the old woman rose up in a fury and shouted, 'I will not be looked at by people I *own*, while I am asleep!' "

"Whew!" Henry rubbed his hand across his forehead.

"So that golden detachment has been bought dearly," Lucy said, thinking aloud. "Actual slavery—for that is what it amounts to—yet inner freedom."

"No," Maria answered, "not perfect inner freedom. Jennifer is detached about everything except this one thing. There she is frozen into the ethos of her generation."

The post-martini exhaustion was setting in. "Human relations . . ." Lucy gave a sigh.

It fell into the silence and stayed there.

"It is not Jack's fault. It is mine," Maria said suddenly. "I am a pig."

"Dear Maria," Lucy felt it strongly, "you are such a darling!"

"I am not a darling. I am a disgusting pig. I am devoured by jealousy of that impossible woman. I hate it that Jack admires her. I always have and I always will."

"So the old record is still playing, is it?" Jack stood in

the doorway, hostile, fatally assuming that what he had heard was the whole truth.

"No, Jack." Lucy got up and went to him. "No, no!" She wondered if she were shouting, and she felt that she could not make him hear. "Maria is sorry. That's what she was saying."

"I'm not sorry!" Maria hurled the words out. And the dangerous spiral, which might have been broken if only Jack had come in a second sooner, twirled itself up again toward misunderstanding and rage.

"Sorry or not, you are coming home now!" They did not offer to drop Lucy off on the way.

"Stay and have some scrambled eggs," Debby said, when she and Henry came back from the farewells, hand in hand.

"I ought to go. I must pack and do a thousand things. . . ." But inertia had taken over and Lucy allowed herself to be persuaded. She felt they had all been in the power of a storm, blown hither and thither on currents they could not control. It had been exhausting and, while Debby could be heard breaking eggs in the kitchen and talking to herself, Lucy lay down full-length on the daybed.

"I feel completely bewildered," Henry said. "What on earth is going on?"

"The quiet groves of academe," Lucy murmured, "the safe groves of academe."

CHAPTER 12

As always when Lucy had had several drinks, she found herself thinking of John, longing for his physical presence, longing to come swinging along a path with his hand in hers as she had seen Henry and Debby do (though John and she had known little enough of such innocent communion), to end the fierce conflict and misery as, no doubt, Jack and Maria would do eventually, in bed. Exhaustion, liquor, the unclosed wound of separation—it was all very well to understand why she was weeping now she was alone in her room, but it did not help. She lay in the dark and felt the cold, comfortless tears slide down her cheeks and into her ears.

It was terribly startling then to hear a sharp rap at the door. In the second that Lucy thought, I can pretend I am not here, she was on her feet, had snapped on the light and opened the door, to be confronted by Jane Seaman, in a trench coat, hatless, and—Lucy suspected—drunk. She looked as if she might fall.

"Take off your coat, Jane, sit down," Lucy said automatically. "I was lying on my bed, trying to get up the energy to undress."

"You said if I needed help . . ." She was still standing on the threshold just inside the door, leaning against it. "I've got to get out of here," she said, shaking her head back and forth like an animal trying to shake off a halter.

Lucy went right over to her and held her, as she staggered forward, then led her to the daybed and helped her out of the coat.

"Why don't I make us some coffee? It won't be very good, hot water out of the tap, but it might sober us up. I've been to a cocktail party, and could do with a little coffee myself."

Jane said nothing at all, just sat there, leaning forward, hugging herself, while Lucy busied herself with Nescafe and paper cups. She sensed that, for the moment, it was best to ask nothing.

"Here you are, Jane. Drink this."

"I feel sick." The voice was thick and muffled, not like Jane's at all.

"Yes . . . well, just take it easy." Lucy poured cold water on a handkerchief and brought it to press against Jane's forehead.

"Thank you. That feels good."

After a moment Jane shakily sipped at the coffee, then drank the whole cup down in a swallow and crushed the empty cup in her hand. "Miss Winter," she said, "I've got to get out of here."

"Yes, I know." Lucy was afraid of saying the wrong thing; her instinct was to treat Jane as a small sick child, wrap her up in a blanket, console her, but this was not possible. The slight figure sitting there, one lank piece of hair drooping over her face, had not relaxed for a moment. "But there is the holiday. Are you going home?"

"Home? I don't have a home. My mother's in Europe and my father wouldn't want me around. He's just married again."

An idea flashed through Lucy's mind . . . ask her home with me. But it was risky, and she decided to wait and see. "Will you stay here then?"

"I suppose so." The tone was flat, as if Jane had come to the end of feeling. She glanced up through her hair defensively. "I only got drunk because I was with such a jerk."

Lucy glanced at her watch. "You got rid of him rather early, didn't you?"

"Yes." The sly smile came and went. "I won't be pawed by a disgusting rich boy who thinks because he has a Thunderbird that he is irresistible."

"Quite. I do see," and Lucy laughed. "My poor girl, you have had rather a lot to take lately."

"I feel like a rat in a cage," Jane said, hugging herself with both arms and rocking back and forth.

"What would you like to do?"

Again Jane shook her head in that obsessive gesture, back and forth, back and forth. "I don't know. Get away."

"You wouldn't get away from yourself." Lucy winced at the smugness of this as soon as she had uttered it.

"I'd get away from *here*."

Lucy wondered what Carryl Cope was doing about this state of affairs, but didn't dare ask. It must be assumed that she had taken on some responsibility for Jane.

"You can't imagine what it is like," Jane said, between her teeth. She looked as if she were full of poison. "Whenever I go into a room, everyone shuts up like a clam; I'm treated like a criminal."

"You would rather have taken the punishment—Oh, I can understand that! But, you see, it would have meant being unable to finish college. That is what Professor Cope wanted to prevent at all costs."

"Maybe she didn't know the cost. Maybe she was only protecting her own skin, not mine."

"Have you talked with her yourself, Jane?"

"Yes, of course," Jane sneered, "she had me in for a little session. She was very kind, blind as a bat, inhuman and cruel without even knowing it."

"That is not my impression of Carryl Cope," Lucy said gently.

"She wants to take me to Europe with her this summer," Jane said, obviously aware that this statement would be startling.

"That is generous."

"No, just guilt."

God, what a mess this is, Lucy thought. How would it ever get straightened out? "I'm going to let that pass, Jane. As things are now you could transfer to another college. Would your father understand?"

"He'd pay the bills all right, if that's what you mean." Lucy felt acutely the desolation of the prospect, the loneliness, the isolation of the girl before her. She took a deep breath and made her decision.

"Jane, would you like to come home with me for the weekend? I can't promise you very much," she went on quickly to give Jane a moment to think the answer over. "But you would be away from here, in New York, and you'd be free to go and come as you please. My mother is often rather dreary now, since my father's death, but she would find it quite appropriate that I bring a student home, and would ask no questions."

Lucy had expected anything except a flood of tears. But the girl was bent over, sobbing great tearing sobs.

"I don't know if that means yes or no," Lucy said gently.

"It m—m—means y—y-yes," Jane wailed. "It's so awfully k-k-kind of you. You're the only kindness."

"Nonsense, I just happen to be here." Lucy waited for the force of the *crise* to spend itself, then she came to the point. "I'm glad you'll come, Jane. Now may I ask just one thing of you?"

Jane nodded.

"If I make an appointment for you with a psychiatrist will you see him? Maybe one way out of the trap is to talk to someone right outside this whole mess, someone who might help you understand what all this is about Carryl Cope."

"I don't need help about Carryl Cope," Jane said as bitterly as ever. "If that's a condition, then, no, I'd rather stay here."

"Of course it's not a condition! But you could do with some help, it seems to me."

"I'm all right."

"You'd be pretty inhuman if you were after these last days. And I don't think you are either inhuman or all right. Hating Carryl isn't going to get you out of the trap, Jane. It's what locked you in there."

Whenever Lucy heard herself laying down the law with such an appearance of authority, she had an immediate reaction of revulsion. It was too easy to stand outside and tell someone off (after all, she herself had just failed in a crucial human relationship); always she had the sense that you kill life by analysing it too rationally. It was a little like taking his shadow away from a person, depriving him of the rich indefinable marsh of feeling from which being springs. The effect on Jane was instantaneous.

"You don't know what you're talking about," she said, with a return of her earlier insolent tone. "You're just like everyone else who has read a little Freud and thinks he can paste a label on things and solve them with a label."

"No nonsense about you, my girl, is there?" Lucy smiled. "You're absolutely right. So why not go to someone who has done more than read a little Freud? Why not go to the horse's mouth?"

Jane got up and walked about restlessly, took a book out of the bookcase, opened it, and put it back. "Reason is all I've got," she said with her back to Lucy. "I'm scared to give it up. They'll want to dig down underneath. I've got this far on reason and I'm damned if I'm going to be dragged back to infancy and go through all that again. . . ." She was crying. "Besides," the words were torn out of her, Lucy felt, "Carryl Cope would call it c-c-cowardice. . ."

"You have to remember that Carryl Cope comes from a different generation. When she says things like that, she is simply reflecting her own background and environment."

"She hasn't failed! What do you suppose would have happened to her if someone had gone around digging in *her* subconscious?"

It occurred to Lucy that if someone had, Jane might not now be caught like a rat in a maze. But it was not the moment to say so. "Maybe she was just lucky, or maybe she has genius that transcends her limitations. Don't you see, Jane, if you run away now from this matrix of pain and conflict, and never come to terms with it, you will just be settling for fossilizing at this stage? Do you really like yourself as you are that much?"

"I'm brilliant. You have said so yourself," Jane said passionately. "I could get my degree at Columbia and go on to the doctorate and become a professor like Cope."

Lucy bit back the answer that leaped to her tongue: Is teaching a profession for the humanly crippled to take refuge in? She said quietly, "Yes, you could."

"But?"

"Jane, may I say a word to you about your long paper?"

"It was good, wasn't it?" In the last few minutes Lucy had watched the artificial bolstered arrogance slip over the suffering human being like a mask. It was not a pleasant thing to see.

"It was a straight A paper. You succeeded admirably in what you had set out to do. But," Lucy paused and fumbled for words, "I found it disturbing. I am sure it gave you pleasure to tell off so many clever people and prove yourself, to yourself, a match for them. But from some absolute view, God's for instance. . ."

"Does God have to be brought in?"

"No, He does not have to be. But perhaps it is the moment to suggest to you that Carryl Cope, who does not believe in Freud, does have faith. This makes her humble on one level, where you are not on any that I can see." The retort was sharp.

"It's faith or Freud then?"

Lucy saw why Carryl Cope had been delighted by this mind. Even drunk, even desperate, the shining intelligence was there.

"There is something a little troubling about brilliance that finds its satisfaction in nay-saying only. You are indulging, Jane, in a corrupting form of power, the power of the critic of critics. I gave your paper an A, as you know, but I liked Pippa's very much better though her grade was a B. Grades are a recognition of accomplishment on one level. Don't be so unintelligent as to overestimate them."

"Don't take away the only thing I have," came the answer, an angry bitter answer.

And Lucy responded with something like anger. "If that's all you have, it's not enough. Not enough for you, not enough for me as your teacher. Your intelligence is, if you will, an angel. You are putting it to poor work for an angel. Really, that paper was full of hatred and self-hatred, hatred of the intellect, hatred of all those critics who can prove themselves superior to the artist they analyse because they can analyse him." Had she gone too far? Jane looked up, met Lucy's eyes and did not waver.

"Yes, I guess that's true," she said, quietly. "You win." Then she sat down, hugging herself and rocking as she had when she first came in.

"Winning isn't important."

"What is?"

"Helping you through this difficult passage is—to me."

"It's humiliating."

"People believe in you. That shouldn't be humiliating."

"I've let them down."

"Yes, you have. You've let them down badly."

"Very well." Jane got up and pulled on her trench coat. "I'll see that god-damned analyst of yours."

They parted on a firm handshake, and on a straight look.

It was a victory, but now Lucy was alone, and she saw that it was after eleven and too late to call her mother, she felt close to exhaustion, and wondered if she had taken on more than she could handle. She had certainly taken a huge risk in making herself responsible for getting Jane to see a psychiatrist. Carryl Cope would resent it. At this moment she envied Carryl deeply—envied her certainties, her eminence, her genius, her faith, even her blindness. I am nothing, Lucy thought with woe, and I have taken on all this as if I were God.

But before she went to sleep, she wondered whether just this were not what you did take on if you chose to be a teacher . . . this, the care of souls.

CHAPTER 13

On the way back to Apple-
ton after the weekend Jane
slept most of the way, and Lucy again found herself looking out the window at the pastures, stone walls and white
farms she had watched flow past her in September, just a
little over two months ago. She would never have imagined
that she would be bringing back a sleeping child, a child
in her care, that she would have found herself already so
deeply engaged and committed. For Jane and she were
coming back *together* and Lucy had determined to make
a real stand, now she was backed up by professional advice. Things could not be allowed to slide along, or Dr.
Gunderson warned that a serious breakdown could take
place.

Fortunately Lucy felt sure that Blake Tillotson would

be responsive, as indeed he was. He readily agreed that
Jane go straight to the infirmary where she could be pro-
tected, and promised to follow through on her father and
if possible get a decision at once that she be given therapy
as Dr. Gunderson had recommended. Lucy had a sense,
for the first time in weeks, that there was hope. But Tillotson then warned her that *"College Notes* will have a rather
vituperative editorial tomorrow. Things have got a little
out of hand," and she agreed to come to a meeting in his
office at four the next day. So, she thought with a sinking
heart, it was too late for the easy solution she had imagined
possible in the euphoria of the return.

By four-o'clock the next afternoon the campus was
buzzing; without mentioning any names or the Seaman
affair itself, the editorial accused the administration of dis-
honesty. It was headed "Justice or Anarchy." Perhaps,
after all, Lucy told herself, a head-on collision might turn
out to be healthier than all the subterranean gossip. Such
were her thoughts as she crossed the campus on the way
to Tillotson's office, and ran into Jack Beveridge.

"Oh Jack, I'm so glad to see you! I'm scared about this
meeting because I've stuck my neck out."

"So have I," he said, his profile looking somewhat nar-
rower, more tense than usual, and the nervous tic back
again around his mouth. "Maria hardly speaks to me."

Lucy received this confession in silence.

"It seems absurd that this ridiculous affair could rock
our marriage, but it sure has." His eyes narrowed. Under

the nervousness Lucy felt suppressed rage. "I sometimes think we've all gone mad. Rats in a cage."

"Odd, that's just the image Jane used."

"Is Carryl invited to this star chamber gathering, by the way? Do you know?"

"Blake didn't mention her name when I talked to him last night." As they walked, Lucy decided she had better inform Jack of what had happened in the last days. "I took Jane home with me for the weekend, Jack. I got her to see a psychiatrist. She's in a bad way."

"You have been a busy little bee!" The tone was teasing, but not kind.

"Please, please, don't be cross."

"I'm not cross," he said testily. "I admire your courage. You have entered the lists as fresh as a daisy, and all the rest of us seem to be worn down by something like passive disgust—with ourselves, I suppose, with the whole messy business college teaching appears to be. I wish I could take Maria to Italy," he said half to himself. "We're rotting here."

Lucy hoped devoutly that Jack's bitter mood would not prevail. Jennifer at least could be counted on, and Blake Tillotson, for some objectivity, some compassion too.

Hallie and Jennifer were already sitting on two of the leather chairs that seem mandatory in presidential offices. Lucy glanced up at the inevitable bad portrait of Miss Wellington in Doctor's robes that stared down at them with an expression of dislike in her pale blue eyes. Miss

Wellington would not approve of psychiatrists, that was sure.

Blake Tillotson came in from his inner sanctum and pulled the chair out from behind the big empty desk with a natural instinct not to be pompous that Lucy inwardly commended.

"Exams are coming up, I know. I realize how precious time is. Let us therefore waste none. By the way," he interrupted himself, "where is Miss Valentine?" And called back into the inner office, "Get Valentine, Pross, will you please?" He had not mentioned the Dean on the telephone and Lucy suspected that he would just as soon she not be found. But she did appear a few seconds later, as polished and composed as an icon.

"Sit down, Dean," Blake said with false cheer. "You know what we are up to, of course."

"The Seaman case, I presume," she said with a fleeting smile.

"Precisely. There are two sides to this question, Jane's and the college's. I am going to ask Miss Winter to brief us on what she knows of Jane's present state of mind. Let us get all the facts on the table before we jump to any rash conclusions."

Lucy felt like a small child who has somehow got herself involved in a grown-up scandal and must present crucial evidence. Jack's teasing remark had put her off, for she had been too busy with Jane's immediate problem to worry about herself having to face a hostile world. Instinctively she turned toward Jennifer as she recounted as briefly as possible the gist of what Dr. Gunderson had told her after his interview with Jane. "I am aware," she ended, "that I have rushed in where angels, notably Olive Hunt, fear to tread. . ."

The laughter helped.

"Thank you, Miss Winter. Now, before I open this meeting to discussion, let me tell you where the administration stands and has stood, and just why." It was clear to them all, as Blake Tillotson spoke, that he had yielded to Carryl Cope's persuasion to give Jane another chance. The degree of resistance to this decision had not been foreseen, he explained, except by Miss Valentine (here he made a slight bow in her direction). At present it was clear that underground resistance was turning into open revolt. Not only had the officers of student government called on him to protest, but also, that very morning, a delegation of instructors and associate professors: "On the one hand we face Jane Seaman, whom a psychiatrist has diagnosed as seriously disturbed, on the other hand, a faculty and student body who, if not seriously disturbed, are certainly up in arms."

"If there were a third hand," Jennifer said, "—but perhaps I must alter the phrase; in the third place, there is Carryl Cope in her embattled eminence."

"Quite." Blake Tillotson did not smile. "Frankly, it's a hell of a mess, and I need your help. What do we do now?"

"We resign ourselves to due process," Jennifer murmured.

Gentle as her remark was, it was greeted with an appalled silence.

Finally Jack spoke. "Do two wrongs make a right? Will backing down now make things any better? And what about Carryl?" His voice rose. "We'll have a free-for-all faculty meeting, delegate someone to call on student government and throw the whole mess in *their* laps. For Carryl, a major humiliation and defeat. And this to be followed, presumably, by the expulsion from the college of Jane Seaman, who is, we are assured, mentally ill!"

"Maybe," Miss Valentine answered quietly. "But the trouble is, Professor, that we have a revolt on our hands."

"And somebody has to be thrown to the lions?" Jack asked icily.

"What is your alternative?" Dean Valentine had, under the circumstances, considerable dignity, Lucy had to admit.

Jack leaned back in his chair, puffing a cigarette.

"Well, Beveridge?" Blake asked a little impatiently.

"It may sound cruel, but if Jane could be shipped right out to a doctor for treatment, I don't see why that wouldn't provide the perfect solution."

"For everyone except Jane," Lucy said. "Surely we can't just wash our hands of her. We do have some responsibility there."

"That," Jennifer said supportively, "is Carryl's strong suit, is it not?"

"In what way are we responsible?" Dean Valentine asked.

The question hung in the air, and when it was clear that it would not be answered, she went on. "The college, as far as I know, has never admitted extenuating circumstances in a case of outright plagiarism."

"Jane could be transferred to another institution," Lucy said. "Surely that is one alternative. . ."

"It would not quiet the storm raised in this morning's *College Notes*, however," Blake said gently. "My own feeling is that whatever is done, can only be done now after consultation both with faculty and students. The thing has gone too far to be hushed up, either by transferring Jane or by handing her over to a sanitarium or its equivalent—provided we could get parental consent, of course—"

"The wolf pack is in full cry," Jennifer answered equally gently, "so we throw it some meat?"

"Very well. You do not approve. What is your own solution?" For the first time Blake Tillotson showed signs of irritation.

"I have none, Blake. I'm in a bad way."

"Why wasn't Carryl asked to this meeting?" Jack's tone was belligerent. If Blake Tillotson had called this particular group together in the hope of getting a dispassionate analysis of the situation, he had been rather optimistic, Lucy thought.

"She is too vulnerable to be dispassionate," Blake answered without equivocation.

"It would seem that we all are," was Jennifer's response to this. "My own view is . . . tentatively . . . (for I must admit that I feel inconclusive), that if education is our business then the only thing that really matters here, or at least the point where our emphasis must lie, is with Jane herself. I cannot help feeling that as far as she is concerned we have bungled hugely from beginning to end." For Jennifer this statement was extraordinarily passionate.

Until now Hallie Summerson had kept very quiet; now she leaned forward, her blue gaze fastened on Jennifer's face, her eyes narrowed slightly.

"I couldn't agree with you more," Blake said at once, "but if our business is education, then surely Carryl Cope also matters."

"Carryl took a chance," Hallie blazed out. "Some of us thought it a risky chance, a dangerous one. I think she must now take the consequences." Alone among them, Hallie seemed sure of where she stood.

"But, Blake, if it could be communicated somehow to the world at large that Jane is ill, mightn't the whole thing just die a natural death?" Jack asked in a gentler tone.

"To be honest with you, Jack, I fear not. Each side is waving the banner of principle now and that means fanaticism. We have got beyond sweet reasonableness."

"After all," Hallie at last drove her point home, "if a general faculty meeting is called, Carryl will have a chance to justify herself. At present she is being smeared outrageously by gossips who don't know what they're talking about." That made sense, Lucy thought. One could count on Hallie's generosity, and she realized that it would have been a serious blow if one could not.

"Very well," Jack said. "The faculty will vote for expulsion, as we all know. Then what? It goes to student government, a bunch of self-righteous girls who are already boiling mad."

"I object," Dean Valentine interrupted. "I have reason to know those girls well. They are not prigs, but they feel —and you must admit they have reason on their side— that this whole affair has made a farce of their authority. Either you have student government or you don't."

"It is not a case where reason noticeably operates," Jennifer said with one of her elusive smiles. "How much of this goes back to Olive, Blake? Perhaps the time has come for us to be painfully frank."

"Indeed, yes. I called on you people with exactly that need in mind. The time has come for honesty with no holds barred, and I think," he smiled his endearing smile, "I can count on this group to provide it." There was a pause while Blake lit a cigarette, a pause he was clearly giving himself before taking the plunge. "As you know, Olive has been pressuring me about our idea that it is time we had a psychiatrist officially attached to the college. You know, too, I expect, that it is a matter of several million dollars. If we carry out this plan, Olive's money will go to Radcliffe." He paused while this news, never so baldly stated before, sank in. "It is no longer easy to raise money for an independent college, especially a woman's college. And it is very easy to take a wholly disinterested attitude when you don't have to do it. If we call a general faculty meeting and the results are what you expect them to be, Jane Seaman will be expelled. This will not prevent her from getting psychiatric care. . ."

"But we shall have washed our hands of her," Hallie broke in. "Blake, how can you?"

The direct attack brought a flush to Blake's forehead. "I am not saying what I shall do, Hallie. I am trying to give you the total picture."

"I am on Carryl's side," Jack said with something like fury. "If I may be forgiven for the professor's tendency to quote, let me remind you of what Yeats wrote on a friend's illness:

'Why should I be dismayed
Though flame had burned the whole
World, as it were a coal,
Now I have seen it weighed
Against a soul?'

Having gone so far, we have no right to throw Carryl and Jane Seaman to the wolves. If you decide to do so, Blake, I'm afraid I shall have to resign."

"Spare us the theatricals, Jack. No decision has been made." Blake spoke sharply; Jack muttered something and subsided.

"On this subject Olive is a little mad, of course." Hallie turned to Blake quite gently, as if to pour oil on the exceedingly troubled waters. "And we all feel for you. But, that being true, won't she be just as angry if we take this whole matter over Carryl's head? It seems to me, Blake, if you will forgive my saying so, that we simply have to forget about Olive Hunt and her millions."

"Hear, hear!" Jack said, too loudly.

Lucy was sorry for Blake, badgered by this group of high-powered individualists, and obviously exerting considerable self-control not to let out his suppressed irritation. He got up and walked over to the windows, then came back and sat down, learning forward. "I would feel very differently," he said, "if any of the solutions before us seemed altogether right. But the hell of a situation like this is that there *is* no good solution. That being so, one looks then for the least damaging to all concerned."

"That is what we did in the first place, isn't it?" Jennifer asked cautiously.

"Yes," Blake sighed deeply. "I suppose we did."

They had been voluble and now they were silent. A glum silence. Lucy felt the room had become a kind of airless prison. They were literally caught.

"But have we considered the possibility," Miss Valentine offered, "that if the whole case is aired, the faculty and student government might vote *not* to expel Jane? We have taken it for granted that they would. I wonder why?"

"Because," Jack said, springing back eagerly to his own position, "there is an immense amount of loose hostility and anger floating around against Carryl and against the kind of power she has exerted."

"Still," Jennifer lifted her chin a fraction, and looked out the window, "I feel we have to take that chance now. We have to defend Carryl openly, if we are to defend her at all."

"I'm inclined to agree with you," Blake said.

He is getting what he wants, Lucy thought, but for the wrong reasons. Should she speak out? "As far as Jane is concerned," she said, taking the leap, "I think I can assure you that she herself would much rather have it this way, a 'normal' punishment rather than the burden of ostracism, the unclarity of her own position."

"Is that so?" Blake asked innocently.

"Good God, Blake, don't you have any idea what goes on?" Jack was really angry now. "That girl has been in hell. No wonder she needs a psychiatrist."

"I may have been stupid, but I do not want to be shouted at, Jack."

"I'm sorry," Jack said, but not with a very good grace.

Lucy felt she was responsible for the truth now. "It is not what happened since the affair broke, it is what made Jane steal the essay in the first place that shows her need for help." She looked anxiously from one to the other of these opinionated faces; even Jennifer looked adamant. They did not want to hear what she must say.

"Do go on, Dr. Winter," the Dean pressed her.

The last thing Lucy wished was to play into Dean Valentine's hand, to justify old animosities, old struggles for power.

"I think I had better not," she said, giving Hallie a desperate look.

"Dear Lucy," Hallie said at once, "I think you must."

And Jennifer added, "Lucy is in an extraordinary position, standing, as it were, in the crossfire. But Blake called us in, I believe, to try to get at the truth, am I right?"

"I had hoped for a discussion that might illuminate the essence, yes," he said, looking depressed. "If you have some ideas about what is really involved here, I must ask you to speak." He turned gravely and earnestly to Lucy. "We could hardly be in greater pain than we are," he added with a saving smile.

"I'm scared."

"Go on," Jennifer prodded gently.

"Well," Lucy swallowed and paused, then began in a rather stiff cold voice, "I think I *am* clear that Jane was put under more stress than she could stand. It looks to me as if she broke down not after the affair exploded, but that the real breakdown was clear in the act itself of stealing the Weil essay, and that she did it as a way out of unbearable pressure." She paused, and heard the intent silence around her. It was frightening.

"You suggest that Professor Cope asked too much of Jane?" Dean Valentine asked.

"Perhaps that is what I mean," Lucy faltered. "It's so very hard to be sure. But," she took the plunge now and spoke quite fast, "there does seem to me a danger in setting such a very high premium on the outstanding student—outstanding intellectually—at the expense perhaps of other qualities. I do feel that it would have been more helpful in the long run if Jane had been steered toward some understanding of herself, and to be a little wary of her compulsive need to excel on one level only. Instead, she was forced like a plant in a hothouse, forced beyond her strength or her capacity."

"Does she herself blame Professor Cope?" Blake asked. No one moved but the tension was unmistakable. Even Jennifer looked drawn.

Justice, Lucy thought, remembering the wind and the snow. What could she say? "Yes, she does. Whatever the basic conflict may be, Jane has projected it there at present. And that means that Carryl Cope is the last person to be able to help her. Perhaps you are not aware that Professor Cope has invited Jane to join her in Italy this summer, with Olive Hunt."

"Carryl has got herself in very deep, hasn't she?" Jennifer murmured, turning toward Hallie with a worried glance.

"Just a moment, please." Blake dominated the group for the first time. "I want to get Miss Winter's full and complete view before we go any further. Your point, as I understand you, is that the college failed in this case by not becoming aware soon enough that she was pushing herself dangerously—compulsively, I suppose a psychiatrist would say? Do you feel that there is an overemphasis on intellectual achievement in the college as a whole? Is that the essence?"

"Oh, I don't know," Lucy answered, quailing. "I'm much too new here to *know* anything of the sort."

Jennifer came to the rescue. "The essence may be that this is the sort of case where a resident psychiatrist would have been apropos."

Blake leaned back, a strange little smile hovering about his lips.

"We are being inexorably driven to the shearing," he said. "Ah, that golden fleece!"

"It is what I have maintained for years," Dean Valentine said.

Jennifer sat up very straight. Her arms gripped the arms of her chair. "If Lucy is right—and she has certainly given more to Jane Seaman, she, the newcomer, than any of the rest of us did or could—if Lucy is right, then a serious attack is being made on the values of this college. We are going to have to do some hard thinking."

"Oh dear," Lucy said, near to tears, "dear me . . ."

"You are getting your baptism of fire all right, my girl," Jack said with a return to his old kindness. "I think it's high time we did some hard thinking. But I just can't see blaming Carryl for having pushed a brilliant student. If Jane couldn't measure up, that's surely not Carryl's fault. Jane's lack of balance probably stems from her unhappy family situation. What's wrong with *us* that we immediately put ashes on our heads and question our fundamental values because one student breaks down? Let's be realistic about this."

"When one student breaks down, it is time to think, nevertheless," Hallie said firmly.

"Yes." Blake got up and walked over to the desk. "Yes," he said again. Then he turned toward them, his kind strained face warmed by a smile. "I think I now have the sense of this meeting at last. With your permission, I am going to call the faculty and present Jane's case in the light of all we have been saying. I shall try to move away from the passions all this has aroused to the big questions that confront us. Thank you, Lucy Winter, for helping us to see our way."

"You will talk this over with Carryl, Blake?" Jack asked anxiously. "You won't spring it on her?"

"I'll talk to Carryl and also to Olive," Blake said decisively. Then he turned to Dean Valentine. "You are kind not to say 'I told you so.'"

"Oh well—" The Dean got up and seemed warmer than she had ever appeared, and more natural. "All things happen in their own good time."

"A sentiment of which Miss Wellington yonder would not approve. She was all for taking the times by storm," Blake said, laughing. For a second they all turned toward the pale cold eyes that stared out of the portrait. Lucy was amused to detect something like a twinkle in them now, or so it seemed, so great was her own relief. "Thank you," Blake turned and shook them each by the hand warmly, "this has been extremely helpful."

But it is he, Lucy thought affectionately, who will bear the brunt of it.

CHAPTER 14

Lucy was surprised and touched when she received a telephone call from Carryl Cope an hour after the fateful faculty meeting.

"We might as well make a tradition of this," her voice had said, "come on over and have a martini. I need one and I suffer from the delusion that drinking alone is dangerous, while drinking *with* someone is safe; the reverse is probably the truth."

"I'll be right over," Lucy said. "I feel shaken."

"Oh?" And Lucy could sense the shadowy smile that accompanied the query. "Well, come along then."

Lucy was glad of the walk. It would clear her head. She was glad of the early dark under the bare creaking branches and the frost-bright sky; at an hour when she could hope to meet no one she knew. The faculty meeting had been a battering, shattering experience. Blake Tillotson had made valiant efforts to maintain a judicial tone, but it had been clear from the start that the anti-Cope faction was in no mood for calm, was determined to air its grievances, now the bottled-up poison could be released. There was talk of favoritism, of power usurped, of special privilege. And unfortunately anger had been met with anger. Jack Beveridge—where had his saving humor fled?—made a furious speech, flagrantly personal, attacking the opposition as "puerile and jealous." He really seemed out of his senses, and it did not help to know that he was probably not so much furiously defending Carryl as furiously attacking Maria. The exhibition had been so painful that Carryl herself had been forced to rise and, with great dignity, set Jack's defense aside as irrelevant. How admirably she had behaved, Lucy thought! There was an example of mastery of stress, all right. In effect, she had abdicated, and because she did so, the final vote and its large majority was possible: the case would be sent to the student council (they were meeting this minute, Lucy realized, glancing at her watch) with a recommendation that Jane be expelled, but with an appending suggestion that there might be grounds for mercy, and that the door be left open for a possible reinstatement after a year. Perhaps, after all the noise and confusion, this was justice. But if so it was a justice so delayed, so poisoned by all that had preceded its definition, that there seemed to Lucy to be no relief in it.

After the vote, there was such a buzz that Blake had some difficulty in getting the faculty's attention and Lucy wondered if, in the excitement of the hour, they realized quite how momentous was the second item laid on the table. For Blake was asking that he be empowered to appoint a committee to look into the question of the appointment of a consulting psychiatrist to advise and counsel the students.

"I shall need your support to get such a suggestion past the trustees. It is a step, as I expect you all know, that they have consistently refused to sanction." And he went on to point out that the Seaman case gave them opportunity for a new attack, since it might be posited that if Jane Seaman had had some help, she might not have been led into such a flagrant act, one which he found himself interpreting (perhaps overindulgently) as having been a cry of distress. "What is your pleasure?"

Carryl asked to be recognized immediately. She stood firm in her well-known view that it was ridiculous to employ a psychiatrist to do what any good teacher should be able to do. "If, as so many of you have made clear that you feel, I am responsible for the present mess, and for the confusion in a student's mind, if indeed I pushed her too hard—and because I too had some inklings of this, tried to defend her *because* I felt responsible—then I see no reason for throwing this responsibility away. I must presume that we are not incapable of learning by our mistakes. If I did not think so, I would feel forced to tender my resignation."

This noble but rationally untenable position was, of course, attacked at once by several of the younger members. There was a roar of laughter when the old Professor of Mathematics rose to suggest that possibly a resident psychiatrist should be appointed to aid and comfort the faculty rather than the students. Jennifer's quiet authority opened the way to the final vote, one hundred and three to five in favor of the President's proposal. He had won the day, and—Lucy could not help thinking—lost the college a few sorely needed millions. How much did Carryl know about this? Everything, of course. How much had she been influenced by what she knew? The safe academic world was riddled with personal affairs, obviously. Passion reduced them all to childishness; it had been frightening to witness Jack Beveridge's disintegration. Was Carryl Cope herself not incorruptible?

Lucy could now see the lights in the upper windows of the old mansion. She felt acutely again the humiliation the faculty meeting must have meant for the woman up there; the little ironies, the overt resentment, these had been met with wonderful grace and self-control, but would there not be a reaction? She rang the bell, feeling dread and something like awe, not toward the famous Professor Cope, but toward the suffering, endearing, conflicted, noble human being. "I love her," she thought, astonished at the intensity of the emotion she was experiencing.

And soon they were sitting again in the same two chairs where they had sat at the first interview so long ago. Carryl, seen against the drawn brocade curtains, looked like an old Cardinal, subtle, worldly, but at the same time, Lucy thought, behind that willed mask like a desperate fox with the pack after her.

"Blake is to call me when the verdict is in. It's a foregone conclusion, of course. But I do hate the suspense, just the same. And where is Jane now?" she asked, leaning forward, holding the martini glass so tightly in her two hands that it looked as if it might break.

"She's with Hallie, or will be after her session with the student council, poor kid. Hallie invited her over for the night. Oh, what a good person she is!"

Carryl sipped her drink, set the glass down. "Yes," she gave a long sigh.

"Do you remember," she fixed Lucy with a bright mocking eye, "when you first sat in that chair, you remarked what a safe little world this college world seemed to you?" She threw back her head and laughed, a loud boisterous laugh with an echo of desperation in it.

"I was a fool, still am. But at least I've learned that it's not at all safe."

"Olive will change her will," Carryl said on the current of her own thoughts. "That's the worst of all this. No . . ." she corrected herself, "Jane and Jane's state is the worst. But that is the next worst."

"Mightn't she change her mind?"

"She might . . . I rather think she won't."

"She is difficult," Lucy said too quickly.

"I can't talk about Olive." Carryl Cope got up and went to her desk.

"I'm sorry."

"Not your fault. Mine. Has it occurred to you that this curious affair has rocked personal lives as well as the public estate?" Carryl was fussing about with papers, her back to Lucy.

"Yes. I suppose you know that Jack's intemperate speech came out of his personal life; he and Maria are at sword's points."

But it was clear by the way Carryl turned and stared that this was news to her. "He certainly cooked my goose, that funny, dear, impossible creature. It's terrible when a New Englander loses his sense of humor; the raw nerve shows."

"It was awful," Lucy assented. "But you were magnificent. I must say I thought you were simply magnificent."

"One can rise to the occasion," Carryl said bitterly. "It's the old ham actor concealed within every professor. But I seem to fall down in the long run." She came back and sat down. "Heaven knows why I talk to you like this." She gave Lucy a piercing glance. "Queer that you should find yourself in the position of a general father confessor. I understand you took Jane home for the weekend; you seem to know all about the Beveridges . . . you are a rather formidable person, Dr. Winter."

Lucy felt miserable under the barb. "I know," she said, blushing furiously. "It's all a mistake. I mean, I just happened to be around when various things happened . . ." The explanation sounded ludicrous, and they both burst into spontaneous laughter. Once she had begun, Lucy simply could not stop. Tears started out of her eyes and she wiped them off, still swept by gusts of laughter. "How wonderful to laugh for a change!"

"I suppose," Carryl said thoughfully when this fit had subsided, "that you were in the position of being able to move about freely among the hierarchies of this semi-fossilized world; fresh, flowing, and human. You know, Lucy, it is a pity that you may not continue to teach. You seem to have a certain genius for it."

"I don't know yet," Lucy answered. "I feel I know nothing about anything, least of all myself. Do you remember saying in this room that first time, 'How are they going to learn anything about feeling if they don't feel?' "

"Heavens, don't quote me to myself. It's too frightening." Carryl smiled, and the smile denied the words; she was pleased. On the wave of her pleasure she turned to Lucy. "I may have put on a good show—one has one's pride—but I find my situation very uncomfortable. You who know so much also know, I presume, just how low my prestige has fallen among both faculty and students . . ."

Lucy did not want to hear this. She found herself putting a hand up to her forehead, shielding her eyes.

"For my sins," Carryl Cope added with a smile.

"Damn them all! Damn them all to hell!" Lucy had been outraged by the smugness of some of the young instructors. The outburst was not an exaggeration of her feelings at the moment, and came as a relief.

"Well, well, Dr. Winter, I think I had better make us a second drink, to calm the savage breast." She got up and stood for a moment, her hands thrust into her pockets. "Of course it does give most people real pleasure to see the mighty fall." And she added over her shoulder, "I do like to give people pleasure whenever I can."

"Don't," Lucy said. "Please don't."

It was as if they had been gliding about fairly happily on thin ice and now had fallen through into black, cold water.

"Don't what? You must allow me to behave badly, my dear Lucy, in this off hour while we wait . . . after all, I have been much too good for my own health. Let the bear growl . . ." and she disappeared down the hall.

Dear bear, Lucy thought, do growl. Anything was better, even this lacerating irony, than the humiliation she had been forced to witness, and could do nothing to alleviate. While Carryl was gone, the doorbell gave an imperious ring, three shorts and one long.

"Oh hell, that's Olive!" Carryl called back from the hall as she went to the door. "The last person I want to see." She looked in at Lucy with a mischievous smile. "Shall we pretend we're not here? No, better see her. After all, you're here to protect me."

"I'd better go." Lucy got up, dismayed at the prospect of acting as buffer under these circumstances.

"Lucy, you must stay!" The tone was imperative.

So she stayed; so she found herself again swept into Olive's disregard of anyone and anything except her present preoccupations; Olive was clearly not pleased to find Lucy there.

"Oh, it's you," she said. "How do you do?" Then to Carryl, "Your stairs will be the death of me." She sat down, picking fluff off her black skirt, agitated, tense, her piercing blue eyes narrowed, waiting for Carryl to come back from the kitchen.

"We were having a post-mortem," Carryl said, handing round the glasses. "I asked Lucy to come over."

"Why didn't you call me?" Olive paid no attention to this remark. "I was waiting for you to call."

"Darling, I figured Blake would call you."

"He did. Drat the man! The courage of a mouse." She gave Carryl a straight angry look. "I warned him, Carryl, and I meant it. I'm not going to give my support to an institution that represents moral cowardice and self-indulgence."

"No one would wish you to do so," Carryl said coldly.

"You're on Blake's side!" Olive got up and stood, back to the fireplace, dominating the room. Old, passionate, furious, wrong, one could not help admiring her just the same, Lucy thought, with a twinge of envy at the kind of freedom women of this generation still had, because they moved from impulse, without *arrière-pensée*, because they did not recognize the meaning of the word "conflict," except in relation to other people. They did not carry it around inside them like some horrible foetus that would never be born. If they were angry, they were angry—and it was someone else's fault.

"I voted against having a resident psychiatrist, if that is the subject of our discourse." Carryl's tone was still icy.

"You did?" The piercing eyes widened. "This young woman, of course, thinks we are crazy old fuddy-duddies who cannot move with the times. But I can't see that fundamental principles change because one student hasn't any guts."

"I voted as I did from conviction." Carryl stood behind Lucy's chair, facing Olive. "But I must say, Olive, I shall be bitterly disappointed if you carry out your childish threat about a legacy to the college. This is a democracy after all, and I mean the college. A vote was taken."

"Childish?"

"Yes, childish. You have a right to your opinion. You have no right to punish other people for theirs."

That, Lucy thought with admiration, is laying it on the line.

"I have the right to leave my money where I choose."

"Indubitably. But if you use money to browbeat people, you are misusing it, Olive. Just as much as I misused power to try to cover for Jane. I have sorely repented of it, I can assure you."

"You were quite right!" Olive blazed.

"No, I was quite wrong."

"You've allowed yourself to be persuaded by a popular

consensus: the majority is always right. I would never have believed it of you, Carryl."

"Live and learn," Carryl said. Lucy felt violently uncomfortable seated as she was, as she always seemed to be, in the crossfire.

"I won't be insulted, Carryl. Please change your tone."

"I'm sorry. I'm tired. This has been rather a nerve-wracking month."

Lucy half-rose, and felt a firm hand on her shoulder, forcing her to sit down again. "No, Lucy, you are not to leave. For heaven's sake sit down, Olive, and let's try to behave like rational human beings." There was an ominous silence. "Please, darling!"

"Oh, very well." Olive Hunt plumped herself down on the little sofa. Carryl drew a small chair forward so she was sitting quite close to Lucy. Together they faced the irate old woman, who now announced, "You won't change my mind."

"Very well, then let's change the subject."

"You are cruel."

Lucy was dismayed to see that Olive was close to tears.

"I am tired," Carryl said again. "Not that that can be an excuse. But, Olive," she said in a patient willed voice, "I think you know where my deepest allegiance lies. If you remove yourself from Appleton—and that in effect is what you speak of doing—I think you must know that you remove yourself from me."

"Is that a threat?"

For the moment Lucy sensed that she was not there,

that she had been forgotten. If only she could slip out un-
noticed!

"It's a reality, for me at least. If it is also a threat, that,
I think, is your affair."

"You're an arrogant fool!"

"And what are you, may one ask?"

"I'm not a coward, anyway."

"No," Carryl permitted herself a faint smile. "No one
could accuse you of being that."

"I'm an old woman." The flash of fire in the blue eyes,
the carriage of the head, the passion in the voice under-
lined the irony. She does not really believe she is old,
Lucy thought, she hates being old.

"I sometimes wish you were," Carryl answered blandly.
"Now, Olive, please behave yourself, darling. After all,
Lucy is not here to take part in or to witness a private
quarrel."

"She rules me with an iron hand." Olive turned to
Lucy, her anger suddenly vanished like fireworks into a
dark sky. "I am absolutely cowed and put in my place.
Don't you think she is intolerable?"

"Olive would have made a great actress. The scene at
Appleton is far too small a stage for her histrionic gifts."
The indulgent, amused tone had come back, and Lucy
knew that, for the moment at least, the danger was past.
"Really, you must think us quite mad, two elderly infants
playing battledore and shuttlecock with a zeal amounting
to fury."

This time Olive joined in the laughter, allowed Carryl

to refill her glass, and looked up at her affectionately. "Well, poor Blake will not consider this a childish game, I can tell you."

Carryl made no answer to this. She was obviously determined to let the quarrel drop, but that this took self-control was evident in the way she walked over to her desk, picked up a book, glanced at it, and slammed it down with a loud thud. "Are you still determined to take that odious girl to Italy with us?" Olive, *enfant terrible*, asked plaintively.

"I wonder . . ." Carryl turned toward Lucy and gave her a keen questioning look. "It would appear that she might not want to go. What do you think, Dr. Winter?"

"Yes, by all means, let us hear the long, long thoughts of youth," Olive said, not unkindly.

"I think it would not be a very good idea," Lucy said.

"Ah!" Olive gleamed her pleasure. "At last we are in the presence of a modicum of common sense. It was a ridiculous idea, as all ideas born of a mistaken sense of guilt are bound to be. The last thing in the world you should do is to go on seeing that girl personally."

"I hate feeling impotent," Carryl answered, walking restlessly about. "There must be something I can do for Jane. Do you really think, Lucy that this psychiatrist chap makes sense? And, by the way, do Jane's parents know about this? Do they approve?"

"I think," Lucy answered warily, "that the idea has been to tell them once the whole case is, so to speak, settled. One's impression is that Jane's father is the big influence in her life, but that he is quite indifferent, absorbed in his second marriage; her mother appears to be totally irresponsible. Oh dear," gloom settled in as Lucy contemplated this unfortunately not uncommon child of the times, "one must admit that Jane has every reason to look for security in the one area where she might be able to grasp it."

"And where is that?" Olive asked. "In stealing other people's work, for instance?"

"In having to excel," Lucy said quite sharply. She felt suddenly exasperated. It was tiring to have to bridge half a century, to have everything one generation took for granted still open to question.

"What did the psychiatrist say?" Carryl asked gently.

It was a legitimate question and Lucy had known that it would be asked, sooner or later. But it was not easy to formulate an answer that would be acceptable to Olive Hunt. Carryl, sensing her hesitation, added, with a mischievous glance at Olive. "I have been thinking that perhaps I should have a talk with this spook myself."

But this time Olive did not rise. She had gone into one of her stances of withdrawal, was sitting with her hands clasped in her lap, and an expression of Buddha-like impassivity masking her face.

"Dr. Gunderson thinks that Jane is seriously disturbed . . . that she has been acting out recently certain ambivalences in her relation to her father, that she has, as they say, projected onto Professor Cope. According to this interpretation—and it makes sense to me—the plagiarism was done out of a subconscious need to be found out, to be punished . . ."

"And so to be released from the pressure I represent?" Carryl asked, coldly. Lucy was all too aware that the very language she spoke, the words themselves, could only be an irritant, if not positively offensive.

"I guess so," she murmured.

In the long pause that followed, Lucy looked anxiously from Olive, who had put a hand up to her face and had apparently not heard, to Carryl, who was sitting forward listening intently, it would seem, to her own thoughts.

Olive gave a hoarse loud laugh. "So, you're a father, Carryl! Very appropriate, I must say."

"Be quiet, Olive." The tone was low but exceedingly firm.

"I must say the whole thing makes me feel quite ill," she answered, her eyes flashing. "But at least if all this folderol has a grain of truth in it, you cannot blame yourself, Carryl. If someone chooses to think you are her father, that is not your fault."

Carryl paid no attention to this, but went on thinking aloud in the compelling way she had when she was really interested. "If your doctor is right, then I should have some understanding about this, for I have certainly tried to be my own father. He died when I was still in college." She addressed herself to Lucy. "He was a scholar of sorts . . . yes, I think one might call him that, though his profession was farming and he had had no education to speak of. Wanted a boy, of course, brought me up to read

Latin and Greek. I wish I could help that girl!" She got up and began pacing the room.

Olive Hunt gave a loud deep sigh, as if she were letting something go, something fall away. Lucy was astonished to see that her eyes had filled with tears. "I hate to be left out of everything," she said. "I hate old age, impotence, self-importance, pride, and all the little subterfuges one indulges in to keep going. Damn it, I suppose I've got to bury my nose in Dr. Freud!"

Was it capitulation, Lucy asked herself, with a wild hope? But just then the telephone gave a muffled ring. They all lifted their heads like animals caught by a bright light in the dark. They waited and heard it ring again, loudly this time.

"At last!" Carryl breathed as she lifted the receiver.

"Yes, this is Professor Cope. Thank you." She was waiting for someone to be put through. "Yes, Blake. Yes . . . Impossible!" She was standing at the desk with her back to Lucy and Olive, who exchanged an anxious glance. What new disaster? They could see her shoulders shaking, and it was clear when she put down the receiver with a triumphant "Thank *you*, Blake," that something wholly unexpected had happened.

"What is it, Carryl?" Olive asked impatiently.

"My dears, I honestly can't quite believe it yet, but Blake called to say that the student council, God bless them, has voted that Jane be allowed to go in peace, that the college receive her back as a regularly enrolled student, as soon as she is well enough. The reason for this mercy? That she has already had her punishment through the long delay and suspension of justice. Who would have believed it of those prigs?" She had been laughing with the triumph, now suddenly she burst into tears. "Pay no attention," she said, "it's just my confounded nerves." She walked round her desk and stood behind it, shifting some papers about on which the tears fell, turning them to put a book back in the bookcase. Neither Olive nor Lucy moved. "What makes one cry," Carryl said in a muffled voice, "is when the young do a little better than one could do oneself, when people come through after all." But the effort at self-control failed. "I think you'd better go, both of you. I've just got to be alone. To *think*," she added with characteristic violence.

"Come along, Lucy," Olive got up, "you and I had better get out."

"Jane, Jane . . ." Carryl murmured to herself, as if they had already gone.

"Think about yourself for a change, darling." Olive used a rough, tender tone Lucy had never heard in her voice before. "Have something to eat. It's *all right*," she said, giving Carryl's shoulders a gentle squeeze of affectionate regard before she turned to go.

Lucy stood at the door, waiting, and thinking ruefully that it was Carryl not Jane who had been punished; thinking, too, that this victory had—as perhaps do all victories where much human suffering has been involved—its after-taste of desolation.

CHAPTER 15

"Let's drive!"

One did not say no to a command of Olive Hunt's, but Lucy felt tired, would have liked to be alone, to lie down on her bed and sleep. As they stood by the car Olive sniffed the air. "It's going to snow . . . December already! Time keeps moving faster and faster. Well, get in!" Suddenly, she was impatient.

"You won't be cold?" For Lucy had noticed the lack of a coat, instead a little old-fashioned fox fur was draped over Olive's shoulders.

"I'm never cold. Heater in the car." She got in and turned some mysterious button. It was a huge black Buick convertible. And, as Lucy had feared, Olive Hunt was an erratic driver. They swooped out of the drive, making

the gravel fly, then came to a sudden halt at an intersection. "Sorry," Olive said, but this was clearly only a
manner of speech. She was evidently one of those dangerous beings who regard a car not as a means of trans-
port but as a means of expression. Neither of them spoke
until they were well outside the town limits on an
empty country road that climbed up and down the hills,
past farmhouses wearing their evening look of warmth and
intimacy so that here in the huge car, propelled she did
not know where, in the power of this alarming stranger,
Lucy felt nostalgia for the small safe rooms they passed
so swiftly, for the quiet of a kitchen stove and someone
knitting in a rocker. She sensed that words were building
up in the woman at her side, and that soon she would be
listening again. Am I always to be an ear, Lucy thought,
exhausted in advance. Why do all these people fasten
onto me? "Outside the hierarchies," Carryl had said. But
Lucy suspected that it was also because she was in-
nocuous, innocent, a kind of receptacle. She represented
the safety of the amateur to whom the professional can
talk. Mesmerized by the road and her thoughts, she did
not have any idea how long this silence had lasted, so
purposeful on Olive's part, so passive on her own. To
what inner destination were they being hurtled through
the dark?

"Thank you," Olive said suddenly.

"For what?"

"For not jabbering."

Lucy laughed. "One can be silent in a car. It's a relief."

"Yes."

Lucy glanced sideways at the profile at her side, the erect stance (no hunching over for Olive Hunt), hands light on the wheel, eyes slightly narrowed, and the line of cheekbone and sharp nose standing out in the light from the dashboard.

"Carryl has outgrown me," she announced. "You know, she's a great woman. Have you ever seen one before?" But she did not wait for an answer. "She's patient with me for old time's sake. After all, we've known each other for twenty years. It grows into a habit." She gave a short laugh. "I taught her a lot of unimportant things—that room, for instance—took her to Europe, gave her an assurance about money and things that she lacked. Never could get anywhere near that shining mind of hers, though. Tried. There, *she* taught *me*, and I had to work hard to keep up, I can tell you. Now that's all over."

"I don't see why . . ." From what Lucy had heard and seen for herself, she guessed that Olive had become something of a burden. But is one not also supported by such burdens? Take the burden away and there is the void.

"No. Too young. You couldn't see. Not yet. How it all ends in despair. No one can hold what they have. It slips through one's fingers. All except money. Money, if you guard it, increases with age. It's the only thing that does."

"What for?"

"God knows!" The answer shot back. "Carryl would say

power. She's right, I expect. Would anybody listen to me if I weren't so rich?" Again Lucy heard the mirthless laugh, like dry leaves rattling. "Now I've had my come-uppance. They won't listen to me. They're going to hire a psychiatrist and Olive Hunt's millions be damned. 'We can't sell our souls,' Blake said to me. The effrontery of it! What has psychiatry to do with souls, anyway, nothing but sex, the sex of infants at that, from what I hear!"

Lucy decided to let this pass.

"The irony of it is that if I had lost all my money in '29, if I hadn't had such very conservative advisers, it might have made all the difference. I might have *learned*," she said savagely. "Too late now. I'm committed. I've taken a stand."

"Yes," Lucy smiled to herself in the dark, "it would take courage to go back on it now."

"Be quiet. I didn't ask you to come on this drive to lecture me!"

"You didn't *ask* me to come," Lucy said, irritated in spite of herself.

"Didn't I?" The car swerved abruptly, throwing Lucy off her balance, and was brought to a halt. They were stopped along the border of a field, a ragged field. The headlights picked out rotten cornstalks blowing in the wind. The silence, after the roar of the engine, was rather too loud. The dark, when the headlights were snapped off, was rather too dark. "I'm tired to death of being myself," the old woman said.

"Oh dear," Lucy answered, "so am I!"

"You? With your whole life before you?"

"Some of it is already past. I was engaged to be married. It has been broken off."

"Oh, you'll marry," Olive said, without pity. "You're young. Everyone makes mistakes, don't you know. I never could persuade Carryl to come and live with me outright. Now it's all over and done with. But I still resent it bitterly. Sometimes I think our love has been nothing but war from beginning to end, war and the binding up of wounds."

"Sometimes I think that's what it was for John and me," Lucy murmured.

"You don't say?" Olive Hunt half-turned in her seat and peered at Lucy through the dark. "How extraordinary . . . I mean, that we should sit here in limbo, you so young, I so old, and meet on such an odd thing as the nature of love." Lucy felt the narrowed eyes piercing her. "Give me a cigarette, child, if you have one."

Lucy fumbled for the cigarettes, handed one to Olive Hunt, and, as she lit it for her, met the fierce blue eyes, and in that second saw the real person tremble somewhere far inside. "But you never felt you were screaming in a high wind trying to be *heard*—with Professor Cope, I mean—did you?"

"Oh, we heard each other all right. Didn't John hear you? I sometimes think men don't 'hear' very well, if I take your meaning to be 'understand what is going on in a person.' That's what makes them so restful. Women wear each other out with their everlasting touching of the nerve. What *am* I saying?" She sounded really shocked. "I must have gone mad. Never thought such a thing, let alone said it in my born years. You have a very pernicious effect on people, Lucy." And she gave a slight fierce smile.

"But I would not have thought that Carryl Cope, with all her brilliance, was especially sensitive in this way, or . . ." Lucy paused.

"Or she wouldn't have made such a mess over Jane?" The old voice came back smartly. "Carryl is like a man, of course. She has been wonderfully stimulating to her students: she has adopted them like orphans, pushed them, wrangled with them, forced them to grow—and they never forget her."

"I'm sure they don't."

"But she has not penetrated to their personal lives or problems. You are right there . . . and a very good thing, too!" There was defiance in the tone. Then she sighed. "But Jane has been different. Carryl loved Jane. You haven't seen her as I have pacing up and down, caged in, worrying about Jane, talking about Jane, planning what could be done after this crisis blows over. It's been a queer lonely time." Olive gave a loud sigh, then puffed fiercely at her cigarette. "I can't forgive that girl. She's responsible for too much suffering."

Yes, Lucy thought, the young always imagine that suffering is their prerogative.

"I think Carryl saw in that girl," Olive went on, "the image of herself when she was young; Jane does have a sort of primary intensity, hunger for work, whatever it is, that one doesn't find every day. And Carryl said to me more than once, 'When that girl is safely launched, I'll retire, Olive.' We were going to take a year and live in Greece." She bowed her head. "Old dreams. Old illusions."

"It's going to be all right," Lucy murmured without real conviction.

"What makes you think so?"

"Well, surely the student council's decision is all to the good?"

"Too late," the old woman said moodily. "My goose is cooked."

"You mean because of this business of the psychiatrist?" She was dying to add, "But you don't *have* to be so stubborn, do you?" and then found that she had uttered the thought aloud. "Forgive me. I didn't mean to say that. It just popped out."

"Pop goes the weasel!" Olive Hunt laughed loudly. "I do have to be stubborn. Don't ask me to change. I can't. I won't."

Lucy restrained an impulse to giggle. It all seemed so absurd, yet was so cruel.

"Dear me," Olive Hunt looked at her watch. "We must be getting back. Carryl might call and wonder where I am." The tone had gentled, but she caught herself at it and quickly added, "She won't, of course. If you think *I'm* stubborn!"

"People are so queer," Lucy said. "I'll never, never understand them."

The car shook as Olive Hunt touched the starter and made the motor roar. "You can say that again!"

Lucy was thinking how from the outside of any relationship it seemed easy to analyse and face reality, but from inside it all got distorted. Only suffering and self-destruction. She had envied the generation that knew so little about themselves that they seemed able to act freely, from impulse. Now she felt it was, after all, an advantage to be at least slightly aware of the irrational forces at work. It kept one from freezing into a "character," from the immobilized nature caught in its own prison like Olive Hunt, driving too fast, speeding back into the coil, the inextricable coil.

"Do you have to commit suicide?" Lucy asked aggressively, because she felt compassion for and also impatience with the old child beside her.

"I like driving fast. It's a relief."

"I didn't mean the driving."

"What did you mean?"

"What drives you to cut yourself off from Appleton and from Carryl. Why must you do it?" Lucy trembled before the storm sure to come. But there was no answer. Only the hands gripped the wheel like claws; the jaw was thrust forward.

"My father would never have countenanced such a thing."

"As a resident psychiatrist?"

"Yes. Inherited money presents certain problems, responsibilities if you will. Perhaps that had never occurred to you, Miss Know-It-All?"

"I don't know anything," Lucy stammered, touched to the quick. "But life does go forward. If people only did what their fathers would have done, the world would stand still!"

"And a good deal more sensible than whirling toward its own destruction, you must admit!"

It's hopeless, Lucy thought, gripping the door-handle as they swung dangerously round a curve at seventy miles an hour. I'm a fool to have tried. After all, perhaps Carryl Cope really wanted this break, and it was Carryl she cared about.

"You're too wise for your own good," Olive Hunt gentled unexpectedly. "You take it all in, listen, make the perfect ear. But what do you do with it? You *did* fight with that John of yours, after all."

"*Touché*," Lucy admitted, swallowing hard. "It's easy to be wise about other people. And anyway, I'm not."

"Oh yes, you are. You used the word 'suicide.' Right on the beam. If I go through with that change in my will, I lose Appleton and Carryl, the two loves of my life. Clear as crystal. Why do I have to do it, you ask? Pride, Lucy, pride. Without it, I'd be committing suicide too. I'm not a person to make idle threats."

They shot through a red light, bypassed an oncoming truck by half an inch, and then heard the sharp, commanding whistle of a policeman as he roared up beside them on a motorcycle.

"Now I've done it!" Olive said, drawing up to the curb with a flourish.

"Listen, dame . . ." (The cap, the goggles, the firm chin; were they turned out on a conveyor belt, Lucy wondered.) "You are a public hazard. Seventy miles an hour through a red light. You go to court, and no argument."

Olive was fidgeting about in her purse, and finally extracted her license, while he waited, unsmiling, pen poised. "My name," Olive said icily, "is Olive Hunt."

"I don't care what your name is. Either you've been drinking or you're crazy. Tell it to the judge."

"Now?" Olive Hunt asked and Lucy detected a slight quaver.

"Tomorrow at ten A.M. at the District Court. This is a Summons. Now, lady, you drive home at twenty miles an hour and pay attention to the stop lights."

Olive started the car and stalled it; Lucy noticed that her hands were shaking. She said a five-letter French word and began again. This time the car crept forward in perfect control.

"That was bad luck," Lucy said. She was rather tense now herself, as if the car had become the symbol for murderous drives within Olive and might run them into a tree.

"My fault," the old lady muttered. "Damn fool! Time I was dead," she added, full of self-hatred and something like despair, Lucy felt. Everything's so ragged and unfinished. Does life really go on tearing at people's vitals forever like some cruel bird of prey? Is there never to be rest or peace, no final and abiding wisdom or fulfillment? Did those who stayed as alive as Olive and Carryl do so because of some flaw, some open wound that never would close? Need? Hunger? Do we die still like hungry babies at the end?

But the car was now drawing to a stop in front of the club.

"Well?" Olive Hunt was impatient to be off. "Here we are. Journey's end . . ."

"Yes," Lucy said absentmindedly, "we have arrived. I must go."

"You could hardly wish to stay incarcerated in this dangerous machine with a daft old woman!" and Olive laughed her mirthless laugh.

"Don't," Lucy said quietly and got out. Then she stood at the curb and watched the car shoot off, throwing hard pieces of snow in her face.

She waved, as one waves to a plane, with no hope that she could be seen but as a form of salute: one could get very fond of impossible people, she thought.

CHAPTER 16

Now everyone flung himself into work with relief; they had all been tossed about enough on the storms of the last weeks. The people who had been most involved even felt an aversion to seeing each other; twice Lucy passed Jack Beveridge crossing the campus—as if by mutual accord they waved, but made no attempt to converse. Jane sent a little note from the sanitarium where she was to stay at least until the beginning of the spring term in February, and for once that articulate nature seemed to be at a loss for words. The careful schooled print marched effortfully across the page, and, after thanking Lucy for "all you have done," ended, "They say I shall get well, and I am trying." Lucy answered this with an affectionate note, and then tried to put Jane out of her mind, though she found that the ironic smile, the lock of fair hair falling over one eye, often swam up between her and the page of a student paper she was correcting, a persistent ghost. It was a relief to be confronted with the fact that the price of excellence could, at least sometimes, prove to be tough-minded balance and hard work: Pippa's paper on Emerson and Thoreau turned out to be more than creditable and Lucy was delighted to be able to tell her so.

"I got so absorbed in it, I forgot about everything else," Pippa said, blushing to the roots of her hair with pleasure. "Though for a while it was like being in a thicket. I had so much material I didn't know how to get out, how to make a plan; I used to sit at my desk and think my head would burst."

"What did you do then?" The way people thought things out had always interested Lucy, how a mind works, process.

"I did what you said. I kept making outlines, discarding wonderful stuff because it wasn't necessary. You said, 'Keep the center clear.' And you said, 'If you get into a panic, spell things out 1, 2, 3.'" The solemnity with which Pippa repeated these simple pieces of advice made Lucy smile. "You smile, but all that helped. Sometimes people take those obvious things for granted, professors, I mean."

"I suppose there's some value in not being brilliant. I can't take anything for granted." Lucy was thinking aloud, at ease with Pippa now. What a long way they had come together in a few months!

"You've taught me a lot."

"Thank you."

"Of course the other thing. . ." Pippa sat on the edge of the chair in the musty-smelling office, as fresh as a daffodil. "The other thing is that somehow doing it for you, I could do it better. It gave an extra edge. I wanted it so much to be good, for you. . ."

"Oh Pippa," Lucy groaned. "Do it for the thing itself, not for me."

"For you as well," Pippa answered with surprising firmness. "Teaching is more than just a subject, you know. It's a person, too. You can't get away from that, even if you want to."

"I do want to—outside the classroom," Lucy said sharply. She had spoken out of her own edginess, out of all that had happened lately, and she had spoken too sharply, for Pippa's eyes filled with tears.

"Come on, Pippa, don't be a goose. I want you to read this paper in class tomorrow. Take it with you. And try to speak up!"

Pippa had risen in response to the tone of dismissal and stood there with the paper in her hands. If she is preparing to burst into tears, Lucy thought grimly, she can jolly well go and do it somewhere else.

"See you tomorrow in class," she added more cordially to Pippa's back as it disappeared down the hall.

You can't win, Lucy thought, taking out a cigarette and puffing furiously at it. There was no avoiding the issue: the most detached teacher in the world infused her detachment, and if one student or another received this as a personal message, well, maybe one had to accept that that was one way of learning. No wonder teaching was called an art, the most difficult kind of art in which the final expression depends upon a delicate and dangerous balance between two people and a subject. Eliminate the subject and the whole center collapses. . .

At this point in her thoughts, Lucy suddenly remembered that she had promised to go to tea in one of the dormitories with a group of freshmen. It was the sort of occasion she most dreaded; but she had accepted at the height of the crisis when she felt that it was important to keep up what contact one could between the faculty and the rebellious student body. Oh well . . .

And a half-hour later she was sitting in one of the parlors that seem to have been designed for just such preposterous occasions—the fancy satin-covered armchairs more suitable for a boudoir in an operetta, the gold-framed mirrors, the old copies of magazines arranged on little tables as in a dentist's office; an atmosphere of being in a waiting room where the shades of all the young men who had sat nervously waiting for a date to come down, the shades of uncomfortable parents falsely jovial, the shades of all the faculty who had been tortured here by feeling themselves under the circumstances neither fish, flesh, nor good red herring, gathered and presided.

"Yes, lemon please and no sugar," she heard herself saying. "Thank you, Nell."

Nell, who did very poor work but always giggled in

conference as if she considered herself hopelessly funny, had now assumed the air of a very stiff hostess who did not know her guests very well.

"It is so kind of you to come, Miss Winter. We have been looking forward to this all week. Oh, I don't think you have met Mary Macaulay."

"How do you do," Lucy said, shaking hands. "Are you enjoying this first year? I expect it must be quite frightening at times. . ."

Mary stammered something and sat down beside Lucy. Two or three girls from the freshman section came in and settled themselves on the floor. Lucy launched one balloon after another—the Christmas vacations and where they would be spent; the snow; the skiing weekend at Dartmouth in prospect, but all these balloons floated off after a second's response and in sheer desperation she asked for another cup of tea, another dry biscuit, and looked at her watch. She couldn't decently leave for another half-hour. What did one do? She was aware that she had been asked to tea because the freshmen enjoyed her class and wanted to know her better. But not one seemed capable of asking a question that might make for adult conversation; as good manners prevailed over life, they sank into a deafening silence. Lucy felt like some sacred gilded animal or relic that is wheeled out on occasion and expected to perform a miracle. What miracle and how? Whatever she was occasionally able to do in class— those moments when she and they were lifted up together on a wave of excitement—was quite impossible here. Here she was simply a rather plain older person saying "yes, thank you" "no, thank you" and deprived of her only valid function in relation to them.

She felt their expectant and already disillusioned eyes upon her; unlike her they had, in their inexperience, looked forward to the occasion, and now they were being disappointed. She was being as natural as she could, but this, she suspected, was just what they did not want. They wanted an intimate contact with the slightly-larger-than-life-size figure who confronted them on the raised platform and through whom (as if she were a Greek oracle) the voices of the gods could be heard. The image made Lucy smile; she caught Nell's amused eyes, and decided to plunge in from there.

"I was smiling because I think this sort of thing is so hopeless," she said. "Don't you agree? It simply doesn't work. Hasn't it ever happened to you—if it hasn't, it will—to invite some really great professor to a social occasion like this, and then have it go flat?"

Two girls exchanged a startled look, then burst into laughter.

"Ah, I see it has," Lucy said, with relief. Now perhaps something could be salvaged, at least the way prepared to save herself and her colleagues from these fatal decrescendos.

"We asked Professor Cope to dinner, and we were so scared no one said a word. She talked the whole time about politics in the Middle East, and none of us knew a thing about it. Oh dear," and they collapsed into delighted giggles.

"What did you expect?" Lucy asked. "I mean, how in

hell could she behave under the circumstances? She was probably much more uncomfortable than you were, as a matter of fact. Here I've been making small talk for nearly an hour and all you do is sit and stare at me as if I were a ludicrous animal. Don't you think you could manage to ask some question that might lead us into a real conversation?" The smiles vanished from the faces and a terrible look of concentrated effort took their place. "No," Lucy said gently. "For one thing we are not brought up in these United States to have the faintest idea of what conversation is. You have led me here like a dancing bear and now expect me to dance without any music—look, we could talk about what has been wrong with the course this semester. That would be really interesting to me."

"We love it!" two girls cried out at once, in alarm.

"You make it all seem so real," Mary said earnestly. "Really, Miss Winter!"

"But you hated Thoreau," Lucy needled them. "Why did you?" At once the atmosphere had become that of a classroom. Oh dear, Lucy thought, there really is no way out. "You know," she said, lighting a cigarette and so giving herself a second's time to think, "I think what you want and think you can get by inviting us to tea and supper with you, just can't be accomplished that way. What you want, I would guess, is to make contact with the human being, with me myself, not Professor Winter. And this is possible sometimes between a student and a professor, but"—Lucy paused and realized that she had now their full attention, and all the masks, the social masks, had been quietly laid aside. "Maybe it can only be done *after* that particular relationship has ended. In the classroom, you see, there are three entities present, you the class, me, and a third far greater than we who fuses us at moments into a whole. When that third is absent, our real relationship falls apart. What we have felt for the last half-hour is that absence, don't you agree?"

Two girls nodded solemnly. Then Mary leaned forward and said, "But, Miss Winter, we like you so much as a person too. Isn't that fair?"

Lucy laughed. "Oh, it's fair enough. It's just not possible to live out the liking in this sort of social situation. I'm being horribly frank with you out of sheer desperation," she ended. "I do think that some true friendships happen *after* a student ceases to be a student. For one thing time telescopes as one grows older—you'll see," she ended, getting up to go. "But for the time being let's settle for what we have."

"Boy, you sure have hit the nail on the head!" A girl Lucy did not know was rubbing her forehead.

"I've simply behaved like a bull in a china shop," Lucy laughed, "if we can change the metaphor. I hope I haven't broken *all* the tea cups in the process!"

She left to a chorus of "Thank yous," escorted by Mary, who shook her hand and said, for once, very seriously, "You made it not just a social situation, so maybe all you said has been disproved after all! We are grateful, Miss Winter."

But the effect on Lucy of the whole episode was to

make her wish wildly for some contemporary to ask her out to dinner and to precede it with a great many drinks. Instead, she saw coming toward her out of the dusk, Maria's determined figure.

"Come for a walk," she said in a tone which precluded refusal. "They told me you were over here."

"One of those nightmarish teas—I hope I managed, by being brutally frank, to scotch any further such invitations."

"You are brave."

"In the absence of any real private life I find I resent this kind of waste of time more than ever before. It's damned lonely at times, Maria."

"Get out and marry your young man."

"I have no young man. I never did have one in the sense that you have Jack." Maria strode along, her hands thrust down into the pockets of her full black coat, like a fury. Only when they had emerged from the campus and turned toward the hill back of the President's house did Maria finally slow down. She stopped then. In the distance the cries of children sledding came to them sharp and clear.

"We are getting a divorce," Maria said in a flat voice.

"Maria!"

"Come on, let's walk."

They walked side by side, with a little distance between them, while Lucy tried to control the panic that was flooding in on Maria's statement. Was everything breaking down, breaking up like an ice-floe under the impact of Jane's own breakdown?

"It can't be true. Wait, Maria . . . wait for this storm to subside."

"It's Jack," Maria said in a hard voice. "He does not change his mind when it is made up. That New Englander."

"But the children . . . Giorgio, Pietro, and Stephen!"

"Don't! I tell you his mind is made up."

"He behaved like a madman at the faculty meeting, like someone possessed, literally possessed by rage. It's not what he really means. Wait, Maria."

"No."

They were climbing the hill, past lighted houses. A woman came to a door and shouted "Mary!" In the stillness, the cry reverberated on and on. It sounded desolate. In its wake there seemed nothing to say.

"We are too different. For a long time we have rubbed each other like a saw on glass. It is enough."

"But you love him!"

"Love is not enough. It does not keep us from murdering each other. It is a love too much like hatred. Even for the boys no father is better than this ugly war. I want to take them to Italy!" She said it with passionate nostalgia. "To Italy!"

"Things are better there?" Lucy asked, out of her own desperation. Was there anywhere in the world where people did not murder each other and call it love?

"Normal warmth, life flowing, natural like the trees and the air. In Italy my sons might grow up into men who love women instead of hating them, men who are not threatened by the power of women. Not in this sour self-devouring world locked in ice," and she kicked a ball of snow forward with one foot as if she hated the very earth they trod.

"It's not true," Lucy stammered. She felt acute distress. Maria, of all people, should not allow herself to be so shaken.

"What's not true?"

"I don't know. How should I? I am just one massive protest!"

"I can't live without love," Maria uttered now, standing with her head flung back as if to challenge the night itself. "I am dying," she announced bitterly, "and I want life and life for my sons. The atmosphere in our house has been dank for weeks now, no air, no sun, Jack's mood like a prison locking us all in to misery and humiliation. I tell you, I will not stand it!" she said to the winter heavens.

"I wonder how many people do . . . live without love. Love comes and goes, but people do manage to go on living somehow."

"I won't live 'somehow!'"

They walked on in silence while Lucy tried to think, but only felt confused, battered, and in some way forlorn, as if she were more closely woven into Jack's and Maria's marriage than seemed sensible. She remembered the first evening she had been in their house, when she had observed a child's painting pinned up on the wall and a bicycle, how warmed she had felt, and how she had said to herself, "Someday I shall have three little boys." But in the world around her lately the only people able to shed warm light were the isolated ones, those 'without love' in Maria's terms, Hallie and Jennifer Finch. Whereever there was passionate love, between the Beveridges, between Carryl and Olive, there was strain, if not hatred, something dark and struggling in the dark . . . herself and John. Only the innocent Atwoods appeared to be immune, and that might be, she surmised, because they had never quite grown up.

"If you go to Italy," she thought aloud, "you will be planting everlasting conflict in the children, surely. They will never be either wholly Italian or wholly American."

"But they will love Italian girls, Italian women, and they will not grow up as Jack did, punished and afraid."

"He was brave enough to marry you!"

"Oh well, people marry in a state of madness. We were like two wolves, starved for each other."

"But when you married him, you must have known whom you were marrying. You knew he was not warm in the same way as you. You must have known!" Lucy felt she was pleading with a goddess of stone. The words bounced back. What offering could one make? What moves such gods as these, the wholly committed who are beaten down? The wholly committed when they have had enough? Not tears, that was sure. Lucy walked fast, paying attention to her feet and to each step she took, to keep the tears back.

"Why are you upset? What is it to you?" Maria turned on her suddenly. "I came to find you because I thought you would be detached."

"I'm not. I can't be," Lucy said miserably. "It just all seems so hopeless . . . you, me, the whole human compact. The waste of feeling."

"Yes," said Maria. They walked on in silence until they had reached the top of the hill. Then Lucy, out of breath, turned to look back, down to the lights of the college and the town, looking so bright and safe, and each lighting up some intimate, tragic struggle. What a farce!

"What possessed Jack to be so involved with these women? I could forgive him, maybe, if this were a sensual passion, if there were some real life in it. What I cannot accept is that he can reject me for Carryl Cope."

"Wait, Maria, please wait!" It was the only word Lucy could find that still rang true. It was preposterous that Jack Beveridge would break up his marriage because of what had happened over Jane. "It just doesn't make sense."

"I have waited three weeks," she said bitterly. "Now, today, I have got our passage to Italy for Christmas."

"Dear town," Lucy said, as if she had not heard.

"Full of good people who murder each other every day."

"Maybe."

"Jack says he can no longer live with an irrational force, an animal, that is what he means. He has placed me in some outer darkness where I can no longer function even as myself apart from him. Can't you see?"

Lucy turned back, as if she were pulled in spite of herself toward the lights, however deceiving they might be, toward the warmth, however false. "He is angry, Maria. His anger will go someday like a fever."

"And meanwhile I shall be dead."

We die between the too-much and the not-enough, Lucy was thinking ironically. She could understand how Maria's excesses, her violence, her absoluteness might be tiring, how living with her one might long for stable, plain, unexciting fare. And yet . . . and yet . . . might one not also hunger for and come to need this torrent of life? "But people don't die of not being loved, only of not loving," she heard herself say. "Look at Jennifer."

"Sacrifice, sacrifice! I want fulfillment, for me, for my children."

"Some people might say that cutting out your heart to find fulfillment was a rather strange thing to do."

Who am I to say such things, Lucy asked herself bitterly? All she wanted at the moment was to be warmed (the wind was icy), to be held close in someone's arms, almost anyone's, she thought ironically, just to be hugged without any words. And she suspected that this is what Maria wanted too, and might just possibly find.

"You are formidable," Maria said after a silence.

"I am desperate," Lucy answered quickly. "I must believe in something, don't you see? Or failing that, have a roll in the hay," she added with a laugh. "Or failing that, a long time in the serene tough world of the intellect, undisturbed contemplation of an idea. Don't you miss teaching sometimes?"

"I haven't exactly stopped doing it," and suddenly Maria smiled. "I think if I ever taught professionally again, I would want small children, eight or nine. They are so fresh." She stopped in her tracks. "Every now and then I forget. Then I remember."

They had reached the town again, and were passing the President's house. Was he at this very moment composing a letter to Olive Hunt to try to persuade her to change her mind? "It will be awfully hard on Carryl Cope if Olive stands by her word and leaves that three million somewhere else!"

"To hell with Carryl Cope!"

"I never did understand what you have against her. It's as if she were a symbol, a gigantic antagonist who I suspect does not exist in reality."

If Maria resented this, she did not show it. She stopped again, and rubbed her forehead with one hand, against the cold, or against the turbulence within. "I know. I am crazy," she said in a low voice. "I am jealous. Black with jealousy of that old bluestocking. It is ridiculous."

"Do you remember Jennifer saying at the Atwoods' that evening how alike you are?"

Maria laughed, a laugh with desperation in it. "Only because we are each a little larger than life-size!"

"I don't understand."

"I am a giant of naturalness and she is a giant of control; we are monsters, each in our own way." Maria looked at her watch. "Good heavens, I must get back. I promised Stephen to go over his arithmetic lesson before supper."

"I'll walk you home."

But the spell was broken, the moment of intimacy gone. Maria was back in her own world, thinking, Lucy sensed, about supper or the immediate task ahead. Her face had taken on its closed somber look. But Lucy was wide-awake still to the issue they had dropped.

"Maria, why do you feel threatened by Carryl?"

"Don't ask me," she said crossly. "I don't know myself." Then she added, "Maybe because she is Jack's ideal. He would love to be like her himself, free of a family, the great Professor Beveridge, aloof on his Olympus. She threatens me as a saint threatens the wife of a man who would really like to enter a monastery." Maria suddenly laughed, as if uttering these words had released some tension in her. "We are all mad—mad—mad—" she said. "Even you!"

"Me?"

"Yes, you, with your impossible love affair, with that John you cannot forget."

"That's not my fault," Lucy said, feeling desolate.

"Oh fault, fault! Nothing is anybody's fault. We are as we are."

"If only we didn't have to hurt each other so much in being it," Lucy murmured to herself. They were at the gate of the Beveridges' house, and she would not go in.

"Thank you for coming," Maria said, quite formal, even shy, as she neared her own domain.

Lucy watched her walk rapidly down the path, and watched the door open and a long oblong of light fall on the path, then black out. It was cold. And it seemed a long way back to the Faculty House.

CHAPTER 17

Lucy walked slowly across the campus to Hallie's the next week in the cold, damp dark, for a pre-Christmas party. She felt dull and tired, as if in the last days some life energy had been drained out of her. But the sheer act of walking roused her and she found herself looking at the lighted buildings all around her with affection; they were no longer pieces of architecture to be judged as insufficient, but intimate presences. She was amazed to think that it was barely three months since she had crossed these same paths on her way to that first tea at Hallie's when she had been so much an outsider; when she was still an ironic observer, and quite uncommitted. Was she committed now? The question had brought her to Hallie's door, where she was greeted with a kiss.

"Here's Lucy!" Hallie announced as if she were bringing them all a present. Lucy shook Henry's hand, then went over to Jennifer, sitting by the fire in the low chair she always chose, and found herself finally standing in the long window with Carryl Cope. Coming from the dark into all this warmth, she felt tears start to her eyes, and turned away from the penetrating glance.

"She needs a drink," Carryl said to the world at large. "Henry is bartender. I can recommend his martinis."

"So here we are again," Hallie was saying. "The last time, Lucy and the Atwoods had just arrived. I remember we teased you. Did you mind?"

"I was vastly interested," Lucy smiled.

"You have had quite an initiation, I must say," Carryl said drily, "you and the Atwoods. You have, one must concede, had a strong dose of Appleton."

"Yes, in three months we have led them rather a dance," Jennifer rested her eyes thoughtfully on Carryl, "haven't we, Carryl?"

"We are not going to talk shop!" Hallie broke in, just as she had before, in exactly the same tone of voice. But of course they did talk shop. Lucy sat cross-legged in front of the fire with her drink, listening to an animated discussion about whom they should invite to give the Tatlock lecture the following year. She listened to the voices, rising and falling, to Carryl Cope's incisive vote against a Harvard luminary, to Jennifer's plumping for Oppenheimer or "someone," as she said, "who has the idea that the most important thing in academic education now is to bridge the split between disciplines." Henry Atwood came in with a suggestion that they consider an anthropologist and preferably a woman. "Anthropology would seem the logical subject to me," he said quietly. Lucy felt that Henry Atwood had moved into new command of himself; he had acquired a kind of authority. "Don't you agree, Lucy?"

"Lucy is not with us," Carryl spoke for her. "She did not hear the question."

"I was just thinking. . ." She had been thinking that she missed the Beveridges more even than she had expected to. Their absence was a presence.

"Listen." Carryl Cope demanded attention, and especially from Jennifer. "You have been keeping the wind from the shorn lamb. But I want to talk about it."

"It?" Jennifer raised her eyebrows.

"I've come to certain conclusions about the Jane Seaman affair and I want to talk about it. Do you mind?" she asked, with a humility and tentativeness Lucy found touching.

"Mind?" Jennifer asked at once. "Mind?" she asked again, swallowing a smile. "You underrate our curiosity."

But the doorbell broke into the prickly moment. Hallie, flustered, rose with a muttered, "Darn whoever it is!" and went to receive the evidently unexpected guests. At once they heard the joy and relief in her voice. "Maria! Jack!" she cried. "You dears. Come in, come in. Henry, get them a drink!" she called back. They all instinctively rose to their feet.

Jack and Maria came in on a cloud of glory. Their faces

were radiant. Even Jack, who smiled so rarely, was smiling as he walked into the room holding Maria's hand. "Well, here we are," he said. "Late but avid. What are you talking about?"

"We were not talking about you. . ." Jennifer began to unwind a long spool of thought, but Jack was too excited to listen.

"No? How extraordinary, Maria! They were not talking about us."

"But," Jennifer proceeded, "we felt your absence. The circle was incomplete."

Maria, as usual, brought her own atmosphere with her. She had been standing in the middle of the room, Jack's hand in hers, and now she left him to go over to Carryl.

"Carryl," she said, "I am glad to see you. You know, you have been in my mind a kind of monster."

"Really, Maria? How odd. For I often seem like a kind of monster to myself."

They shook hands. Nobody laughed, though Lucy felt an almost irresistible desire to giggle, as she did on all self-consciously formal occasions, as she had years ago when two members of her class had destroyed a plasticene map and hurled bits of it at each other, only to stand eventually before the assembled school and solemnly shake hands. These two had been hurling bits of the map of love at each other for some years. It had its humorous side.

"Here you are." Henry, as usual oblivious to the stress and triumph of the moment, brought filled glasses to Maria and Jack.

"Well, we can sit down," Hallie said. "We really do not have to stand any longer."

"We do not have to if there is another chair," Jack said.

"Oh Henry, do bring one in from the dining room, like an angel!"

They were all waiting for the moment to coalesce, waiting for what Carryl had been going to say. Could she say it now the Beveridges had come?

"What was it you were all discussing when we so rudely interrupted?" Jack asked. It was hard to define how he looked, somehow glistening, a swimmer through magic airs. And he bowed over Carryl's hand like a magician as he lit her cigarette.

"Thank you, Jack. Our lights have been somewhat obscured lately, haven't they?" She gave him one of those half-mocking, half-tender looks that Lucy had come to recognize as the prelude to a pounce.

"Possibly," Jack said with a fleeting smile at Maria.

Then with a sudden imperious gesture Carryl took one of his hands in hers and reached over to Maria with the other. "It's all right? The tiger is tamed?"

Lucy though, Oh dear, she can't resist!

"Yes, if Jack is the tiger!" Maria said instantly and laughed with a perfectly happy laugh. It rang out in the room like a largesse, like a fling of golden sunlight poured over them.

"Yes, if Maria is the tiger!" Jack answered.

"You wretch!" Maria whispered as he went past her, back to his chair, but she was smiling.

"'Teach me to heare Mermaides singing, or to keep off envie's stinging, and finde what winde serves to advance an honest minde,'" Jennifer recited in her softest voice, the one that always gathered silence to it. When had she said it before in just that tone?

"Yes, Jennifer." Carryl leaned forward, was suddenly serious. "I have been thinking about that *winde*. . ."

"We all have." Hallie spoke into the fire. "The secret society we chaffed these newcomers about bust right open." When Hallie was moved, she was apt to use rather old-fashioned slang, Lucy had observed. "Well, and now where are we, Carryl?"

"Right in the middle of something," Carryl answered, and she added with distaste, "It's all been so immensely personal, for one thing . . . so disastrously personal. Somehow or other we are stripped down."

The words sank into a silence. For once, Lucy thought, we are silent.

"Yes. . ." Maria gave a sigh, and it too rested there, like a question and an answer.

They had finished their drinks, but no one moved.

"It's really preposterous that one girl's *dis*honest mind could cause such an earthquake!" Jack said, then turned expectantly toward Carryl, who was evidently preparing to speak.

"During all these weeks, feeling your censure. . ." She made a gesture to quell any attempt to refute the last word. "No, don't deny it! All these weeks, I have been trying to come to terms with this thing." The earnest tone changed to a mocking one, and she shrugged. "Oh, I don't suppose any of us change very much, nor shall I. Sooner or later one comes to terms with oneself."

"You are quite splendid," Maria said firmly. Lucy would have liked to hug her. One thing about wholehearted people like Maria was that their positive was as definite as their negative. "It is a kind of splendor for which I have felt great jealousy."

"Not really?" Carryl turned to her in honest bewilderment.

"Of course."

"Why?"

"Your brilliance stands on rock, the rock of real achievement. If anyone is Appleton, you are it. Why do you think I have been jealous?" Maria threw back her head, and her eyes sparkled. She seemed wrapped in her own splendor of physical being.

"If so, there is something very wrong with Appleton," Carryl answered without smiling. She had withdrawn, hooded like a fierce old bird that will not leap into the air except for good cause. For a second she closed her eyes. When she opened them she spoke to Lucy. "I refused to recognize the whole person in Jane Seaman. Why?" She was obviously asking herself that question. "The little devil came and went in my house as if it were her own. And I justified this invasion on the grounds that she had a hungry mind, and if I could nourish it I would."

"Didn't she?" Jack asked. "I would have thought that estimate accurate."

"Maybe, but she did not come for the books, or to nourish her mind. . ." Carryl said wearily. "She came for me. She came for help. And I was not there. Help was not forthcoming." She sat there, glittering with self-castigation as if it were a jewel she wore.

"But," Jennifer answered gently, "who knows what would have happened if you had given her what she wanted. . ."

"Ah! The risk," Carryl nodded. "Yes, the risk . . . and we are back again at the price of excellence, which is, if I remember, where we came in."

"And it is?" Jennifer probed.

"Why not the joy? Why the price?" Maria almost shouted. "Why do you all talk in terms of sacrifice, never of fulfillment?" It could not have been more startling if a gigantic flower in fireworks had burst there in the room and showered them with sparks.

"Yes," Lucy asked, in passionate recognition, "why always the *price*?"

"Because," Jennifer said quite harshly, and without equivocation, "we have—haven't we, Carryl?—come to equate excellence with some sort of mutilation."

"This I cannot see," Maria came back at once. "This I do not understand. This," she said, looking down and not at Jack, "has nearly broken my marriage in two."

"Because," Hallie stood up in the force of her conviction, "because what we give our students, whether we are personal with them or not, is the marrow, the essence of ourselves, what true lovers ask of love—and what does this mean? It means that for one reason or another, we are ourselves cripples. We are able to give so much just because we do not have."

"No!" Maria said, shaking her head vehemently. "No!"

"No what?" Carryl Cope turned the full force of her person toward Maria like a searching beam of light. It was the moment of truth. They all felt it.

"No, you give from richness, not from poverty, from wholeness or not at all."

"You are not a teacher," Jack said, as if to protect the others.

"I was. I know what I am talking about. Lucy knows too, she still knows because she has not yet been poisoned by this atmosphere of self-mutilation, and she has been able to lead at least one of her students into excellence—I am speaking of Pippa—because she did not withhold herself."

"Henry, make some more martinis," Hallie whispered.

"But you are willing to grant, surely, that there is such a thing as the *life* of the mind?" Jennifer asked. "It seems to me that we are talking round and round the same nub, and the nub is the 'life of the mind' and how it is nourished, or stimulated. I am not so sure," she said, obviously launched on one of her long ruminations, "that the awareness we have—we who have chosen or been forced to remain old maids—of what might be called mutilation is not a perfectly healthy sign. Surely we do not wish to hold ourselves up as examples? Are we not the way rather than the end? It is not our function to lead the honest mind necessarily to venture upon our path, but to find its own—and these paths must be different. I do not myself see Appleton as primarily a school for scholars. If it were, we would have to reduce the enrollment by ninety per cent."

"As a school for what then?" Jack asked.

"The total human being!" Lucy said fiercely, "and doesn't that mean to learn to think about feeling as well as about everything else—and how are we to teach that if we don't know ourselves?"

"Great teachers are great people. You can't get away from that." It came from Debby Atwood, she who had been so silent.

"And there are as many kinds of great people as there are hummingbirds in Brazil, four hundred to be exact." Jack turned from the group toward Carryl, and for the first time this evening his slight stammer was in evidence. "C-Carryl, it's very noble of you, and all that, to feel responsible for Jane, but I doubt, actually, if it would have been such a very great help if you had given whatever it was you think you withheld. After all, you have had a thousand successes against this one failure. Look at that mathematical girl, the genius we have around, she seems to be doing fine. And I very much doubt whether she is pouring out her soul into Professor March's unwilling ears. Haven't we all gone a little wild over Jane?" He turned to the others now. "The trouble with Appleton is that we take it all too seriously. . ."

"Hear, hear!" Maria clapped her hands.

"Damn!" Carryl said. "I no longer know what I think . . .

or feel." She turned to Henry, standing in the doorway—jug in his hand, "yes, give me another drink." Then she added, half to herself, it seemed, "The fact is that I was more involved than I should have been in Jane's success—and failure."

On these words a silence fell. Jennifer stretched out her hands to the fire. Maria got up and asked Jack for a light, then bent down to kiss him on the ear. Hallie disappeared into the kitchen. It was, Lucy felt, like an intermission at a play. And while it went on, she considered the whole conversation as if it had been a jigsaw puzzle with one after another of them fitting in a piece. But somehow the whole pattern was still not clear.

"Thank you, Henry," Carryl said as he bent over to fill her glass. "We know what you do very well, but we don't know what you think," she looked at him with her quizzical dominating look, "you who are intoxicated by Appleton!"

Henry gave a desperate glance toward his wife. He stood there with the martini jug in his hand, taken by surprise.

"I'm bursting," he said, "but I don't know quite with what!"

Then the saving laughter seized them all.

"Come on, Henry," Jack teased when the laughter had subsided, "you have the floor. And we are not going to let you get away with such imprecision. Collect yourself, man. Think, Henry!" His voice mocked the professorial.

"I can only speak for myself," he said. "I've never met a

problem like Jane, thank God. All I know is that I don't get all this withholding business. It seems to me you just teach and then go away and hope some of what you said sank in, and then when you see the papers you know almost none of it did. As far as I can see, teaching is as much as anything the ability to handle failure most of the time, one's own failure, I mean. . ." He stood there, waving the jug back and forth a little as if it were a ball in his hand. Then he set it down on a side table.

One simply could not be ironic about Henry, Lucy thought. He was too innocent and clear.

"Once in a while you do have to, kind of, be a father to somebody, though. Do you remember Saul, Debby? This boy used to hang around all night until I was propping my eyes open." He laughed. "Saul wasn't even bright."

"And you were a good father?" Carryl asked gently.

"He had the patience of a saint," Debby answered from, as usual, the floor. "And Saul did pass!"

"Now he writes me twelve-page letters and says no one understands him but me." Henry rubbed the back of his head.

"Henry, you are a darling," Maria enunciated for them all.

"It's only because I listened to him that he thinks that," he said, his eyes bright behind his glasses.

"Yes. . ." Jennifer had been silent for a long time, and was still concentrated on the fire, feeding it tenderly with pine cones and little pieces of kindling. Now she lifted her head. "I have a hunch that we are at last, with Henry's help," and she turned to give him one of her rare smiles, "coming close to the point. We are all verbalizers by trade"—Lucy recognized in the pause the beginning of one of Jennifer's slow elucidations, the spider beginning to weave her web—"and so we tend to believe that everything is communicated through words. But do we actually reach our students by heart-to-heart *talks*?" She raised her eyebrows. "I myself have never done such a thing in forty years. No, we teach a subject to half-formed people who are, we must presume, going to grow into wholeness partly through the discipline of exploring a subject. But . . ." and here she accelerated her pace as she turned to Carryl, as if she had been afraid she would be interrupted and must get to the point, "there is an intangible communion between a teacher and a student which is not, I am prepared to grant, wholly intellectual."

"Obviously." Carryl sounded impatient. "What are you after, Jennifer?"

" 'Teach me to heare mermaides singing. . .' " she went on, imperturbably. "Perhaps quite simply you did not hear the mermaids singing, you and Jane."

"It is not usual to hear mermaids singing while studying the trade routes of the Middle Ages!" A ripple of smiles acknowledged Carryl's answer, but it was clear that it had been an interruption and the web was by no means woven to the end.

"Don't break the thread," Lucy murmured.

"It is a very long fine-spun thread," Jennifer smiled,

"but I am coming to the end. Carryl, you did, I think, withhold from Jane Seaman one element in your discourse, and it was crucial."

"What element?" Carryl asked, on the defensive.

"We are speaking of something withheld which is essential. How could you imagine that you were withholding what you perhaps felt deeply? Yet failed to communicate, though you gave Seaman the run of your library. . ."

"What in hell did I withhold then?" Carryl was close to anger now, a lion caught in a very fine-spun web. "What more am I supposed to give? Time is the most precious thing I have and I gave Jane endless time, time I could not afford, time that should have gone into that long overdue essay for the Seaton Festschrift, for instance."

Perhaps they all felt as Lucy did that they should not really be present while these two fought it out.

"You withheld love." Jennifer finished her web.

Carryl did not react at once, either with anger or with recognition. Then she clasped her hands between her knees and smiled her faint ironic smile. "Yes, that was the one thing I was afraid to give. You may be right at that, Jennifer. You usually are."

It was handsome. It flashed through Lucy's mind that if Carryl had been more detached she would not have been afraid. It was, she considered, not so much a failure of love as a failure of detachment, but enough had been spoken.

"And you wonder why Henry finds Appleton intoxicating." Jack moved in to break the tension. "After infinite gyrations, we sometimes manage to reach the simple truth."

"No," Maria broke in. "No, Jack. No irony, please. We are all afraid, aren't we?" she said, and now everyone was rising to his feet. Maria's arm slipped through Jack's. "Aren't we, my fierce withholding tiger?"

"Yes," Jack said, and yes was clearly a very big word.

"Good heavens, Jackie, it is nearly eight! The children will be starved and burning up the furniture in the fireplace or some such thing!" Then—for all was now a chaos of departure—Maria moved across to Carryl and threw her arms around her. "Darling, you are not a saint, thank God! But you are wonderful and we love you. Don't we, Jack?"

"We honor you, Carryl," he said with a queer little bow.

Carryl extricated herself from Maria's embrace and was, Lucy was delighted to observe, blushing for once in her life. "Oh, what a funny evening," she said, crossing the room to say goodbye to Hallie. "Thank you, Hallie." Then she turned back to the others. "Well, you Atwoods and Lucy, perhaps now your initiation is complete. As usual, it turns out to be an anticlimax: we have certainly taken our hair down in this small room."

Dear room, Lucy thought, dear room, and dear, tormented, *great* people. Her thoughts were interrupted by Carryl's commanding, "I'll take you home, Lucy!"

CHAPTER 18

They sat in the car, where Carryl had drawn up, at the Faculty Club entrance. It was one of those timeless moments when ease and intimacy are possible; Lucy sensed that it was not inappropriate to take out a cigarette and light it, as if the gesture were an unspoken 'yes, let's talk.' She had been wondering, as they drove along, what it had cost Carryl Cope to expose herself and to be exposed in the last hour. It had not seemed quite in character, somehow, had seemed rather a deliberate act of the will, a kind of penance. Why?

"Why did you do it?" she uttered when she had drawn a long puff on her cigarette.

"Self-punishment, no doubt. Also, I have discovered lately that I care rather more than I had supposed about what my colleagues think of me. Also pride," and Lucy saw the pride flash out, as she struck a match to light her cigarette. "I did not want to be judged without being present at the judgment."

"Jane is going to be all right," Lucy said.

"Is she? I suppose she is now paying a psychiatrist to give her the love that I withheld." The tired bitterness of the tone did not escape Lucy.

"She is going to a psychiatrist because of love given or not given long before she met you, Carryl."

"Yes, no doubt—infantile deprivations or guilt. Why do we feel so guilty, all of us?"

"It's the human condition."

"For once you sound pious," Carryl said impatiently. Lucy clasped her hands together miserably. "No. It's only because I feel inadequate . . . and," she hesitated before the word, "lonely, I guess. It looked two days ago as if Jack and Maria were through, but they have made it."

"You wouldn't have been happy with that stiff-necked young man," Carryl pronounced.

"I expect not. But I miss him." She changed the subject because she was afraid she would begin to cry, and this she imagined was the one thing Carryl Cope would find intolerable. "Oh dear, people's strengths are so inextricably woven into their weaknesses. What about Olive Hunt?" she asked.

"Olive is punishing herself, God knows for what. She has cut herself off from me, from the college. She too withholds. . ."

There was a silence while each, Lucy surmised, was thinking of the other's problem.

"Come along!" Carryl roused herself, "Come along home with me. I'll make you scrambled eggs and coffee—it's all I know how to cook, but it's better than going back into that dismal hole." And she started the engine.

"Much better," Lucy murmured.

An hour later they were sitting opposite each other by the fire having a second cup of coffee. "I have the strangest sensation," Lucy said, "as if I were coming back all the time."

"Back where?"

"Well, at Hallie's for instance, it was coming back to the room where I first met you all, feeling so new and strange. Here I am coming back, too. I've never told you what it meant to be invited up here when you asked me that first time."

Lucy looked hard at the wall of books, at Carryl's great desk piled high with papers, as usual, at the Constable clouds over the mantel. "Those clouds . . ." she murmured.

"Ah yes, the clouds." Carryl glanced up at them coldly. "Olive will no doubt come and recapture them one of these days." She drank down the end of her coffee with relish. It was impossible to tell what she was thinking.

"It's a very grand room," Lucy said. Lucy was acutely aware at the moment of the intensity of the life lived here; of its stature; of its continual self-creation, and of its essential solitude—and by contrast, she saw herself as naked, homeless and vulnerable as a newborn mouse.

"Grand?" Carryl shrugged. "Olive's grandeur then, not mine."

"No, yours. It's the life lived here. It's what you are."

"Oh well," Carryl shrugged again as if she were shrugging off all the accretions of time and position, "when one is old, as old as I am . . ." She reached for a cigarette and went on talking without taking it out of her mouth. "I don't really care a hoot about all this. What I care about is doing some work at last. And I might do that better in a cell." Then she lit up and drew a long puff. "One of my fantasies is to be locked up in jail for a year, with a table, a chair, a bed."

"And a good many books surely?"

"Yes, I suppose jails have rather poor libraries on mediaeval trade routes, so that's out."

"But you will be going to Europe this summer?"

"Yes . . . no . . . I don't know," and she puffed furiously at her cigarette again. "Did it ever occur to you, Lucy, that the machinery of feeling can wear out? They call it metal fatigue, I hear, when a plane suddenly blows up in the air. This business of Jane has taken something out of me for good. Olive . . ." She let the name rest on the air between them. "One comes to the end."

Lucy felt unable to speak. What could one say?

"I really do have work to do," Carryl repeated half to herself. "Have some more coffee."

"Don't move. I'll get it!" Lucy was glad of the chance to escape the unwavering yet impersonal gaze, for Carryl had been staring through rather than at her, and it was unnerving.

"Still," she went on thinking aloud, "it is strange to unweave the strands of so many years. The silence," she said. "Olive used to interrupt me a dozen times a day. The phone sometimes rang every five minutes. . ."

"Yes, the silence," Lucy said in a small voice. Desolation filled her. It seemed an eternity since she had heard an intimate voice. Carryl's absent gaze suddenly focussed.

"Poor child," she said quite briskly. "But you know of course that there will be other voices, other people. You will not be lonely forever, whatever you may think now. I, on the other hand, am glad to be rid of it all, to know that there will never be another voice pulling me away from one self into another. I feel lighter . . . free . . ." But as she spoke, she looked older than Lucy had ever seen her, old and tired. Her eyelids drooped over the keen eyes. For an instant Lucy wondered if she were falling asleep . . . wondered too if when the vital energy is gone, and one is free, the imagined work ever gets done.

"Freedom could be frightening."

"Not to me!" And Carryl sat up, fiercely awake. "I've wasted too much time. I have five books in me still . . . at least." Lucy caught the hint of bravado.

"What makes you so sure Olive won't change her mind?"

"She may, but I shan't. I have said, so be it, *ainsi soit-il*: when you have said that, and mean it, you're through. You've gone."

"I wish I could say it," Lucy said miserably.

"Cheer up," Carryl said with a return to her old tone of light mockery. "*Tout passe, tout casse, tout lasse*, as the

French are fond of reminding us. Even grief . . . though that may be the hardest thing to accept." Then she gave Lucy a long friendly look, so intent that Lucy found herself shielding her eyes with one hand. "I suspect that this tragic affair has helped you to grow up. The unswaddling of the ego, if I may put it that way, is exceedingly painful, of course." Then she got up and took a different tone. "Will you stay on here? I suppose you are aware that you have made an impression. I have an idea that promotion is in the air . . . just an idea, mind you."

But instead of relief, Lucy felt only disturbance, fear. "I don't know," she said, "I never told you that I only got my Doctor's degree so as to be able to stay in Cambridge while John was at Medical School . . . I don't know," she said, prickling all over with anxiety at what this confession might provoke, "I guess total commitment to teaching, when I feel so unsettled in every other way, scares me."

Carryl did not smile. And Lucy sensed the something pitiless, like steel, in the small definite woman standing across the room against a wall of books. "Extraordinary," she murmured, "a Harvard degree, and for such an odd reason."

"Love does not seem odd to a woman," Lucy bristled. "It did not seem odd then," she corrected herself.

"And now?" The hawk pounced.

"I don't know. It would seem the logical thing to stay."

"People do not stay at Appleton to teach because it is logical," Carryl Cope said coldly.

"Why do they?"

"Because a fire burns in their heads," Carryl said with a snort. "Why else? It would have been logical for me to go to Columbia, but I am here."

Lucy got up and stood facing Carryl across the room. In this position, at least she felt less dominated.

"And why?" Carryl asked and answered her own question. "Because I felt challenged. Teaching women is a special kind of challenge. Most of the cards are stacked against one."

"Yes," Lucy said. "I have seen that. I do understand what you mean." But she still held herself back.

"All this talk about the price of excellence has a grain of truth in it as well as a grain of salt, Lucy."

Lucy forced herself to stand her ground, as if this were some sort of final examination she could not afford to fail. To fail what? To fail whom? My life, my self, she thought. "I was with Maria when she shouted Joy, Fulfillment against you all. I'm not sure I would find absolute joy and fulfillment in teaching."

"Absolute joy?" Carryl hooted. "You *are* young, *Doctor* Winter! Partial joys, partial fulfillments, we are lucky to get them in this world."

"Oh hell," Lucy capitulated. "You know very well I love teaching here. But it's my whole life I can't imagine without . . . without . . ." She could not finish. But at least she could hold the tears back.

Carryl came right across the room and laid a hand on Lucy's shoulder and cocked her head. "Well, nobody wants you to dwindle into teaching as Millamant dwindled into marriage. Of course it's not to be your whole life, you silly fool!" She gave Lucy's cheek a tap and threw herself down in the red armchair. "People who are rooted in work are rooted in life," she said, "you know that as well as I do. But that doesn't mean those roots never flower."

"I want to belong somewhere, to be someone," Lucy said, amazed at her own violence.

"You belong at Appleton if you want to. And you are certainly someone. Why do you suppose we've all talked to you the way we have? Of course, the trouble with women is that they're all of a piece. Just because that odious doctor doesn't want to marry you, you've forgotten who you are."

"A little white house like Hallie's, a garden . . ." Lucy laughed harshly.

"And a hundred Pippas and Jane Seamans to plague you and challenge you and make you grow up, willy nilly."

"I can't see it yet, Carryl, but I'm on the way. Give me time," Lucy said.

"I have time. You do not," Carryl answered relentlessly. "Moments of decision pass like beauty itself . . . and you are beautiful, you know, beautifully undecided, beautifully needed, beautifully yourself. I am drunk," Carryl veered, "and it is time I took you back."

Lucy was grateful that she had not said "home." "You have been very kind."

"I am very old."

"No, very complete."

"God forbid!"

"It is good about the Beveridges," Lucy said, as she got into her coat.

"Yes."

"Jane is going to be all right, Carryl."

"Yes, I expect she will."

"And Olive?"

"Olive is suffering. It is her climate. In another week she will begin to learn Russian or Chinese. Olive is alive."

"And you . . . and I?"

"You and I?" Carryl thrust her hands into the pockets of her old leather coat. A cigarette dangled from her mouth. She looked faintly raffish. "You and I? Well, we may not be all right, but we'll survive."

"Yes," Lucy smiled, "we'll survive." Though all she felt at the moment was exhaustion, she said again, "We will survive, you and I," and then she found herself kissing Carryl Cope like a very old friend. "If I stay," she added, as they started down the stairs, "it will be for love."

"All right," Carryl laughed, "you win!"

"I think you have made me fall in love with a profession."

"Because a fire burns in my head?"

"Because a fire burns in your head."

Beyond Desire by Sherwood Anderson

Dark Laughter by Sherwood Anderson

The Example of Melville by Warner Berthoff

The Garretson Chronicle by Gerald Warner Brace

Sixteen Modern American Authors edited by Jackson R. Bryer

Adventures of Huckleberry Finn by Samuel Clemens (Norton Critical Edition)

Fig Tree John by Edwin Corle

The Red Badge of Courage by Stephen Crane (Norton Critical Edition)

Sister Carrie by Theodore Dreiser (Norton Critical Edition)

Soldiers' Pay by William Faulkner

Return to Yesterday by Ford Madox Ford

Bloodline by Ernest J. Gaines

Emily Dickinson: The Mind of the Poet by Albert J. Gelpi

The Blithedale Romance by Nathaniel Hawthorne

The House of the Seven Gables by Nathaniel Hawthorne (Norton Critical Edition)

The Scarlet Letter by Nathaniel Hawthorne (Norton Critical Edition)

Moby-Dick as Doubloon edited by Harrison Hayford and Hershel Parker

Form and Fable in American Fiction by Daniel Hoffman

The Dynamics of Literary Response by Norman N. Holland

Poems in Persons by Norman N. Holland

The Ambassadors by Henry James (Norton Critical Edition)

The Awkward Age by Henry James

Eight Tales From the Major Phase: "In the Cage" and Others by Henry James

The Portrait of a Lady by Henry James (Norton Critical Edition)

The Turn of the Screw by Henry James (Norton Critical Edition)

The Arts in Modern American Civilization by John A. Kouwenhoven

The Ugly American by William J. Lederer and Eugene Burdick

The Comic Tradition in America: An Anthology of American Humor edited by
   Kenneth S. Lynn

Hawthorne's Tragic Vision by Roy R. Male

The Confidence-Man by Herman Melville (Norton Critical Edition)

Moby-Dick by Herman Melville (Norton Critical Edition)

Interviews With Black Writers edited by John O'Brien

Character and Opinion in the United States by George Santayana

Mrs. Stevens Hears the Mermaids Singing by May Sarton

The Small Room by May Sarton

The Journey by Lillian Smith

Gertrude Stein's America by Gertrude Stein

Paris France by Gertrude Stein

Walden and *Civil Disobedience* by Henry David Thoreau (Norton Critical
   Edition)

Cane by Jean Toomer

The Novel of Manners in America by James W. Tuttleton

Eight American Authors edited by James Woodress, et al.

IN THE NORTON LIBRARY

Aphra Behn   *Oroonoko, or The Royal Slave* (a novel) (Introduction by Lore Metzger)   N702

Margaret Llewellyn Davies, editor   *Life As We Have Known It*, by Co-operative Working Women (Introduction by Virginia Woolf)   N772

Margaret Fuller   *Woman in the Nineteenth Century* (Introduction by Bernard Rosenthal)   N615

George Gissing   *The Odd Women* (a novel)   N610

Margaret Jarman Hagood   *Mothers of the South: Portraiture of the White Tenant Farm Woman* (Introduction by Anne Firor Scott)   N816

John S. Haller and Robin M. Haller   *The Physician and Sexuality in Victorian America*   N845

Karen Horney   *Feminine Psychology*   N686

Raden Adjeng Kartini   *Letters of a Javanese Princess*   N207

Ruth Landes   *The Ojibwa Woman*   N574

Alan Macfarlane   *The Family Life of Ralph Josselin, a Seventeenth Century Clergyman: An Essay in Historical Anthropology*   N849

George Meredith   *Diana of the Crossways* (a novel) (Introduction by Lois Josephs Fowler)   N700

H. F. Peters   *My Sister, My Spouse: A Biography of Lou Andreas-Salomé* (preface by Anaïs Nin)   N478

May Sarton   *Mrs. Stevens Hears the Mermaids Singing* (a novel) (Introduction by Carolyn G. Heilbrun)   N762

May Sarton   *The Small Room* (a novel)   N832

George Bernard Shaw   *An Unsocial Socialist* (a novel) (Introductions by Barbara Bellow Watson and R. F. Dietrich)   N660

Kathryn Kish Sklar   *Catherine Beecher: A Study in American Domesticity*   N812

Julia Cherry Spruill   *Women's Life and Work in the Southern Colonies* (Introduction by Anne Firor Scott)   N662

Barbara Bellow Watson   *A Shavian Guide to the Intelligent Woman*   N640

Mary Wollstonecraft   *Maria, or the Wrongs of Woman* (a novel) (Introduction by Moira Ferguson)   N761

Mary Wollstonecraft   *A Vindication of the Rights of Woman* (Introduction by Charles W. Hagelman, Jr.)   N373